The Messiah Covenant

Book Three:
The Mikveh Scrolls

Steven G. Lightfoot

Word Ghost Press

ISBN: 0615967329
ISBN-13: 9780615967325

Dedication

Dedications are the last words I write when completing a book. I find it interesting that they are typically the first words that are read by others. It's as if the reader is seeing the end of the story before they even begin. Well, maybe not the story per se, but definitely the motivator, the muse, the inspiration behind the story.

So, I dedicate this book, as I have the previous books in this series, to my motivator, my muse, my inspiration... my beloved wife, Angela. Not only has she lived through the creation of this narrative, but simultaneously, along the way, she has walked with me on my discernment path into pastoral ministry as a Methodist Pastor, advanced in her own career, and raised our teenagers to be successful adults. To say that I am blessed by her is so very understated. She has been, <u>is</u>, continues to be, the light of my life. If I am *Geoffrey Proudman*, it is only because, all of this time... she has been my *Angelica*.

Foreword
by Brittany McReynolds

*"My hope is built on nothing less than Jesus' blood and righteous-
ness; I dare not trust the sweetest frame, but wholly lean on Jesus' name...
When he shall come with trumpet sound, Oh, may I then in Him be
found; dressed in His righteousness alone, faultless to stand before the
throne. On Christ the solid rock I stand, all other ground is sinking
sand, all other ground is sinking sand." –Edward Mote*

Nearing the start of our first term as missionaries, my
husband, Dane, and I find our lives focusing, as if the lens of
a microscope, upon the person of Christ; He becomes clearer -
His heart, His character, His vision - while all the rest becomes
blurred peripherals. We are preparing ourselves to risk everything, to live a life that costs us much, because the name of Jesus
is not simply demanding of it, but because He is *worthy* of it.
Who is more deserving of a love that gladly and willingly gives
everything should circumstances require of it, than the very
person who displayed the ultimate love by giving everything,
once and for all, for us to live? And not being satisfied to supply
life, but to supply life *abundant*! Everlasting life, redemptive life,
sustaining life.

What hope! And you will not find this in any other religion. Christianity is unique in this fact; that Jesus died, not end-
ing with that, but being raised from the dead and ascending to
be with the Father, defeating death on our behalf; and it does

not stop there, for we have been given a promise. He is coming again; Jesus is coming for his bride, he has gone to prepare a place for us.

> *In my Father's house are many mansions; if it were not so, I would have told you. I go to prepare a place for you. And if I go and prepare a place for you, I will come again and receive you to Myself; that where I am, you may be also. (John 14: 2-3)*

He is faithful, faithful to the end. In my own life I have seen it, and in the lives of many others. His promises are sure. They do not fail us like the words of men often do. Our hearts can be fickle, and our words mere flattery. But the Lord, when He speaks, speaks always in truth and in love, and when He promises He will always follow through. When Jesus spoke those words, he meant every one of them. "I will come again and receive you to Myself," he said. Do we believe it? Do we truly trust that he will return for us, His beloved? His bride? I can proclaim without hesitation that I most certainly do! Never in my life has he failed me. The Lord is incapable of doing anything but what is for our highest good, and that will always be in the form of what brings us to the end of ourselves and closer to Him.

In Genesis God called Abraham to a land He would show him. And what did God tell him? "And I will make of you a great nation, and I will bless you and make your name great, so that you will be a blessing. I will bless those who bless you, and him who dishonors you I will curse, and in you all the families of the earth shall be blessed." (Gen. 12: 2-3) And from that moment onward God has been working tirelessly to bring that promise to completion, because He is faithful. Issuing forth from the line of Abraham is a lineage leading to the one man that can save us all. He is the ultimate blessing to all nations, to all the families of the earth. His name is Jesus.

Let us therefore, dwell for a moment upon this beautiful truth. As we stand apart from God we are sinners, and as such we are incapable of having relationship with God the Father. And yet, as scripture so wonderfully puts it, "God shows his love for us in that while we were still sinners, Christ died for us." (Rom. 5:8) I do not know of any love greater than this. It is a good enough thing, and rare indeed that someone would lay down their life for the sake of someone they deeply care for, who is good and honorable; but to lay down one's life for someone that is by all accounts not even worthy to be called good... that is another thing altogether. And Christ does it for us all. The righteous and the unrighteous alike – all have been given the opportunity for redemption and reconciliation with the Father. And again we have this promise, that for those who have chosen to live in obedience to God, to allow him to be Lord of their lives, He will return and receive them to Himself. He is coming for his bride.

On my wedding day, I remember the excitement of anticipation. Counting down the final minutes until I would join my love at the altar and commit myself to him, and him alone, for the rest of our lives, I've never felt time go so slow and so fast all at once. And suddenly there I am, walking down the aisle, and all I can do is gaze upon this beautiful man who is waiting eagerly for my arrival, with eyes only for me. There, before God and before our friends and families, we vowed to spend our lives choosing to love each other; under any circumstance choosing for the highest good of the other. The nervousness, the excitement, the overwhelming sense of affection – racing heart, sweaty hands, uncontrollable tears and laughter – all at the same time, and the beauty of it all. It's something that even these words do little justice to convey unless you yourself have experienced it.

I can only surmise that if I am able to feel all of that for the man I love, then on the day that Christ returns it will be magnified more than this body could bear. As much love as I have for my husband, and he for me, pales in comparison to the love Christ has for his bride. On that day trumpets will sound, the heavens will open, and it will be the most beautiful wedding ceremony the world has ever seen. On that day, we will go to the place he has prepared for us, we will be reunited with the Father, and we will be so overwhelmed by His glory that as the angels circling round him have done for eternity, surely the only words we will be able to sing will be "Holy, holy, holy, is the Lord God Almighty!" Praise God! I have been washed by his blood, I have been made new, a pure and spotless bride, and I cannot wait for the day that he comes to marry me.

Author's Note

I rejoice in the Lord, and give Him all glory and honor and praise that this project has culminated in this third (and final?) book of <u>The Mikveh Scrolls</u> series. For several years now, this series has been a central focus of my outreach effort; my attempt to fulfill my Lord's mandate to make disciples for the kingdom. And what better way to end this endeavor than by embracing the subject of Christ's return for His Church.

Matthew's gospel account gives us some essential information concerning the return of our Lord for His bride, the Church. The disciples approach their Master, who is sitting on the Mount of Olives, and they say to him, *"Tell us... when will this happen, and what will be the sign of your coming and of the end of the age?"* (Matthew 24:3)

Jesus answers them with a detailed explanation, which includes the following sound advice: *"Therefore keep watch, because you do not know on what day your Lord will come. But understand this: If the owner of the house had known at what time of night the thief was coming, he would have kept watch and would not have let his house be broken into. So you also must be ready, because the Son of Man will come at an hour when you do not expect him."* (Matthew 24:42-44)

Because only God the Father knows when He will dispatch His Son to gather His children up to Him, we must live each day, each and every moment, in full expectation that, in the blink of an eye, we could hear the blast of the trumpet, and be spirited away to meet our Lord in the air, just as scripture foretells.

Knowing that we do not know the hour of His return, makes the work we do now, spreading the gospel message to people near and far, all the more urgent. As Brittany so capably put it in her *Foreword* narrative, we must focus our lives, "as if the lens of a microscope, upon the person of Christ." Everything else is of no consequence as compared to readying God's people for the journey home. The urgency is great. There are far too many in the world that need Him still; their souls are in danger of being forever lost, and time is so very short!

I find myself torn between selfishly yearning for His immediate return and hoping for enough time to offer the hope of Christ to just one more lost soul. It's the continuous conundrum of the evangelist: desiring Christ's return while praying for one more day to preach the message of salvation. In our clinic ministry to the poor and the sick, I see spiritual suffering manifested as medical maladies every day. Lifestyle choices become illness. Illness breeds hopelessness. Hopelessness produces anger, regret and spiritual bankruptcy. It's a vicious cycle; but a cycle that is easily broken by the power of The Name... Jesus. The remedy is the blood of the Lamb of God, which takes away the sins of the world! Jesus is the cure.

What you may not realize is that you don't have to be a pastor or a missionary to be a minister of the Word. You too can be an evangelist and bring the message of hope to a hurting and broken world, and you need not travel to far-off exotic places to have an impact! You can be a light for Christ right in your own community. The Body of Christ needs international missionaries, like Brittany and Dane, my daughter and son-in-love, in the remote regions of Asia. And, as a father, I could not be more proud of (and more humbled by) their sacrificial devotion to their Savior. But not everyone is called to or equipped for hiking the Himalayas. Equally essential members of the Body are needed to work in the domestic mission fields across America's communities. You can have a tremendous impact for the kingdom right in your own sphere of influence... If that's your calling, and rest assured we are ALL called to spread the good news, pray that God would use you for His purpose and watch Him go to work creating Divine appointments for you; placing people in your path and giving you the opportunity and the courage to share the message of salvation.

I know, from witnessing the great examples of Christian motherhood and devotion to family, as demonstrated by my wife, Angela, and my daughters, Brittany, Michelle and Meghann, that evangelism takes many forms, not the least of which is the testimony offered through the example of a Christ-centered life. These high-powered women of God speak volumes to the unbelieving world in the way they live their faith, unapologetically and transparently, every single day, in the midst of their communities. I know the power of that testimony, because it has inspired this old war-dog over the years, even to the point of surrendering myself, after more than a decade avoiding the call to pastoral ministry.

So, beloved... while we wait with hearts full of expectation for our Lord to come, we must remember that we are not alone in our wanting, and that we have a job to do while we wait. *"The Spirit and the bride say 'Come.' And let the one who hears say, 'Come.' And let the one who is thirsty come; let the one who wishes take the water of life without cost."* While we wait, let us not rest, but rather let us present ourselves as vessels full of living water, ready to pour out on any and all who thirst. In Jesus' name!

chapter

ONE

For you have made the LORD, my refuge,

Even the Most High, your dwelling place.

-Psalm 91:9

HELL. THREE YEARS SINCE *THE GATHERING.*

Abaddon sat, spirit dashed, pasty-pale head pressed in clammy hands, on his massive rock throne. Involuntarily, his fingers traced and stroked the heads of the snarling, carved-stone hellhounds flanking his seat. On other occasions, the smooth coolness of the obsidian on his fingertips somehow soothed his angst; but not today. Hell's Great Hall stretched before him into the blackness. The faint, anguished wails of the damned drifted up from the Abyss, but even they did not give him the usual satisfaction. In the grand scheme of things, all was on schedule: Despite the many saved souls harvested at *The Gathering,* the nations were embracing false religions at an ever increasing rate; the demonically-influenced Universalists' multi-path approach to attaining heaven was rapidly becoming the prevailing dogma of many professing Christians; feel-good false teachers in modern mega-churches were tickling the ears of seekers, filling their heads with the prosperity gospel, leading them down a path devoid of the message of salvation through Christ; a new resurgence of Islamic terrorists was wreaking havoc on civilized society; and, the secular humanist world-view was busily inducing cultural suicide in the western world, successfully infiltrating and emasculating what was once the earth's last bastion of God-inspired liberty - the United States of America. Abaddon, Satan, as the people knew him, ruled humankind.

By all accounts, Abaddon should have been gleeful regarding the state of the world, but the crushing defeat he had suffered in the Hinnom Valley at the hands of the Reverend Geoffrey Proudman, Doctor Simon Cross, and company had vexed him. They, by their steadfast faith in Christ, had snatched his revenge away, casting him back to Hell like a lower echelon demon. And what's more, Proudman had branded his forehead with the image of the crucifix – a mark even he could not remove with all of his supernatural power. Even now, he could see its reflection in the surface of the black igneous glass upon which he sat. It mocked and tormented him as it blazed red on his pale-white forehead. He would live with it through eternity;

a constant reminder of his failure and subordinate position in the spiritual realm. If he didn't feel so low, he might be enraged. If he had any sense of motivation, he might rise again to seek blessed revenge. But, the thrashing he had been dealt had simply sucked the passion out of him. His disposition was such that he actually preferred wallowing in the stench of his pitiful existence to expending any more energy on doing evil. His colossal ego was bruised and he'd just assume close up shop.

NEW COVENANT CHURCH, HOUSTON, TEXAS.

The Reverend Geoffrey Proudman watched the torrential downpour from his office window. Ordinarily he liked the rain, but it was a cold Sunday morning and that meant light attendance in the services, especially with rain of this magnitude accompanied by rolling thunder and frequent streaks of lightning. Usually thunderstorms provided a comfortable working atmosphere for Proudman, allowing his creative juices to flow. On stormy days he often did his best writing, as if the storm ushered in to his mind a keen awareness of the leading of the Holy Spirit. This storm seemed somehow angry and malevolent, however, with lower-than-normal, heavily brooding clouds, forked flashes of enraged lightning and violently shuddering thunder.

With a little more than an hour until the first service, Proudman pulled himself from his mesmerized gaze out the window. The strobes of livid light had a hypnotic effect on him and it was by sheer force of will that Proudman broke from his trance. He eased into his leather desk chair, a wedding gift from his beloved Angelica. Each time he nestled into it, her image came to his mind, causing a smile and familiar warmth to envelope him. He touched the wireless mouse on his desk and the computer monitor awoke from its temporary rest. "Just a few finishing touches and this one is in the bag," he said out loud. A few keystrokes later and his Sunday sermon was complete. Proudman looked the work over one last time before committing it to the printer, which whirred to life and began pushing crisp white paper through its inner mechanisms.

Proudman spun in his chair and execu-glided across the office floor, coasting to the side-table where his wireless printer industriously produced his sermon notes. He tapped on the top of the printer, as if his tapping would shorten the wait time by making the printer labor faster. As the final page motored onto the printer's deck, Proudman snatched the papers up and glided back to his desk in a graceful motion, made so by countless hours of sermon writing and repetition. He ceremoniously tapped the papers vertically, and then horizontally, and then vertically again, lining up the edges perfectly before folding them once and tucking them in his New American Standard Study Bible, precisely marking this Sunday's scripture reading. He then rested both hands on the Holy Book, closed his eyes and meditated on the cross, just as he had done countless Sundays before. After a few minutes of silent prayer, Proudman prayed audibly, "Holy Spirit, I invite you into this place. Use me as an instrument for the will of the Father; move me out of the way and let me speak as if I am speaking the very words of God. Let all who hear, receive what you need them to hear. In Jesus' name I pray. Amen." As Proudman concluded his prayer, a low guttural rumble rolled from the storm outside his window. The lights in the office dimmed as the electrical power waned from a lightning strike near the power grid. As the church's systems stabilized, he rose from his desk and moved toward the door leading to the sanctuary, muttering a prayer under his breath for the lights and sound equipment to survive the storm.

Proudman entered the sanctuary as the worship team cranked up their version of Israel Houghton's *"Say So."* He joined Angelica, Missy, Freddie, C.P. and Alex on the front row. They were already launched into full-praise mode to the upbeat music. The five-hundred plus congregation sang out with hands raised and clapping, *"Let the redeemed of the Lord say so! Let the redeemed of the Lord say so! Let the redeemed of the Lord say so! Say so! Say so!"* Proudman turned to look at the sanctuary auditorium. He praised God for the full seats and the joyful worshippers who had braved the foul weather. How much the church had grown and how quickly, he thought. "I used to know everyone's name when we first moved in here," he spoke into Angelica's ear, "but now there are just too many new faces!"

"I know, right!" Angelica spoke back into his ear. "Proud of you!"

"It's not me. It's God!" Proudman pointed upward as he replied.

"I know. But I'm still proud of you!"

Geoffrey Proudman smiled at his beautiful, energetic Angelica. He laughed inwardly as he watched her dance to the music. If there was music, her rear was moving! Proudman loved that about her. He knew in his heart that there was no way he could have stayed the course on growing New Covenant Church without her by his side. He was the spiritual leader, but she had the business sense and the people skills to make the church viable. And, she was no slouch spiritually; leading Bible studies, small groups, women's retreats, and leading worship from time to time. He was grateful and thanked God for her daily.

As the worship team concluded their set, Proudman ascended the platform from the side steps. "Thank you praise band! Good morning saints!" The response was mediocre at best so Proudman repeated with more vigor, "GOOD MORNING, SAINTS!

"GOOD MORNING, PASTOR!" they responded.

"That's more like it! Let's come to the Lord together in prayer this morning!" Proudman raised his arms and bowed his head, signaling the congregation to follow suit. "Abba, Father... we praise Your Holy Name. We praise You for Your sovereignty and Your control over all that is in our universe. We ask Your Holy Spirit into this sanctuary, which has been set apart from the world for Your honor and glory. Open our hearts and minds and prepare us to receive all that You have for us this morning. In Christ's name we pray. Amen. Please be seated."

The congregation settled into place and as the rustling subsided, Proudman smoothed his notes out on the podium, glanced at them briefly, and then stepped to the side of the podium and began to preach.

"Advent is a season of expectation and hope. We celebrate the first advent or 'coming' of the Christ Child, and we hope for the second advent, the second coming, of Christ the King. It is a time when we look for deliverance from the struggles and strife of the world and set our eyes on the light of Christ. We hope for peace... not only for peace in our surroundings and in the world, but for peace within.

When I was a younger man, leading Marines in combat in the deserts of Kuwait and Iraq, I found myself looking for peace in the midst of chaos; on a cool December night, in a fighting hole dug deep into the desert sands of the Kuwaiti border.

The ground war was imminent and the atmosphere was intense, with SCUD and FROG missiles impacting in our vicinity and the whoosh of outbound HAWK and PATRIOT missiles launching to intercept or retaliate. As we sat in our holes, with nothing to do but wait and reflect, every man was faced with the reality of his own mortality and with the knowledge that soon we would be breaching the minefields that lay between us and the liberation of Kuwait. Not a great place to spend Christmas.

At that time in my life I knew about Jesus, but I didn't know Him personally. I also knew that I had a responsibility to lead my Marines, and that responsibility included getting them through the war with mind, body, and spirit intact.

As I sat in my fighting hole with several of my men, I could see the anxiety in their faces. I could also see the vastness of the night sky above with stars in such magnificent abundance that it brought to mind a Christmas card that I had seen when I was a child... with the magi in the desert following a bright star set in a sea of blackness. It was one of those foil cards and its shimmering image captivated my imagination. There was comfort in that memory, but there was conviction too.

I pulled a field Bible out of my pack and opened it to Psalms. It wasn't long before I came across Psalm 91, and as I read it the part that especially spoke to me was this:

> *⁵ You will not be afraid of the terror by night,*
>
> *Or of the arrow that flies by day;*
>
> *⁶ Of the pestilence that stalks in darkness,*
>
> *Or of the destruction that lays waste at noon.*
>
> *⁷ A thousand may fall at your side*
>
> *And ten thousand at your right hand,*
>
> *But it shall not approach you.*

⁸ You will only look on with your eyes

And see the recompense of the wicked.

⁹ For you have made the LORD, my refuge,

Even the Most High, your dwelling place.

¹⁰ No evil will befall you,

Nor will any plague come near your tent.

The sense of peace that came over me was as powerful as anything I had ever experienced. I was so overcome with the sense of it, that I read the entire Psalm out loud to my Marines. Some wept silently. Some stared quietly up at the night sky. But all felt the sense of peace, peace within by the power of the Holy Spirit. Gone were the faces of anxiety. As I made my way around the perimeter, visiting with each Marine in their fighting holes, sharing the Psalm, the same peace was apparent.

Now this is just my opinion, mind you, but I think that one of the first steps in salvation, in my experience anyway, is the surrendering of self and the allowing of the peace of Christ Jesus to enter your heart. That experience in the desert paved the way for my becoming a Christian after the war. That advent season, for me, was the peaceful beginning of a season of expectation and hope, which ultimately led to the coming of Christ in my life.

Psalm 91 will forever be deeply ingrained in the meaning of advent for me. It represents all that I know about the promise of hope, of light and of peace... deep internal, down-to-your-soul peace... that only comes, by grace, from the Prince of Peace: Our Lord and Savior Jesus Christ."

Proudman sensed that he was finished with his sermon. He could feel his cheeks were wet, but didn't recall at what point he had begun to cry. The congregation sat motionless, not wanting the atmosphere to dissipate. Clearly, the Holy Spirit had taken the sermon and run with it. Angelica wiped the tears from her face with a tissue from one of the boxes strategically placed all around the auditorium for just such an occasion. Everywhere people did the same as they sat quietly thanking Jesus for showing up in such a moving and power-ful way. In the quiet, the chirping of crickets could be heard, driven into the building by the downpour. The *chirp chirp chirp* slowly entered Proudman's consciousness and he began to chuckle. "Do you hear that?" he whispered. "It's crickets chirping. That's a preacher's worst nightmare... to preach a sermon and get nothing but crickets in response," he contin-ued to whisper. Giggles and chuckles bounced around the au-ditorium as the people heard the insects chirping and under-stood the comedic circumstances that had developed around them. "Crickets!" Proudman laughed. "Actual crickets! You can't write this kind of comedy, folks!" All around the church, chuckles and giggles turned to outright laughter. Proudman caught his wife's eye and smiled at her. Angelica smiled back. How blessed they both felt in this moment.

❦

Baal entered the Great Hall quietly so as not to give Abaddon any reason to unleash his fury on him as was so often the routine whenever Abaddon felt interrupted. "Master," Baal said softly as he approached the throne, bent in a submissive posture, eyes to the ground, "is there anything you require?"

Abaddon glanced up through his fingers, not really wanting to take his head out of his hands, and wished he could ignore his annoying second in command long enough that he would just go away. "Stop the pitiful groveling, Baal. It really is so unbecoming. And, no... I don't require anything except to be left alone in my misery. Why must you bother me so? Shouldn't you be down in the Abyss torturing an atheist or something?"

"Master, I only wish to serve. And, of course I am... we are all... concerned..."

"Concerned? How bloody touching. Concerned about my well-being, are you? Isn't that nice that you and the rest of Hell's minions are 'concerned' about me? Well you can all rot in... well... you can all go straight to... oh, bugger off, Baal. Really, just leave me before you anger me. I'm too miserable to waste energy on being angry."

"Lord, perhaps you have forgotten what day it is? Perhaps, my Lord, you might remember that on earth some half century ago you planted a seed for just such a time as this!"

"What are you going on about? Imbecile! What is this nonsense to which you refer? Well, out with it, man! Get to the point!"

"Master, the son is poised for greatness. It is time..."

NAIROBI, KENYA. DECEMBER 1960.

Anwar Muhammad Abasi poured himself another glass of Changaa and leered at the young, white anthropologist sitting at the table in the corner of the dingy establishment, busily thumbing through pages of notes. With a lustful eye he traced her body while the cheap liquor chiseled away his impulse control and built up a false wall of courage. Courage was not something that came naturally to Abasi. A mid-level official in the Kenyan government, he had risen to his highest level of incompetence. As a Muslim in a predominantly Christian nation, and as a member of the mostly Christian Luo tribe, Anwar Abasi was a man with a questionable, if not bleak, future. His career path was flat-lined and his luck with the ladies was equally dead.

He blatantly watched the woman sip a bottle of tepid cola through a straw, eyeballing her lightly colored lips as they pursed and drew the brown liquid into her mouth. Abasi grabbed the Changaa bottle and his just-poured glass and slid side-ways off the bar stool, sloshing his drink onto his pants as he did so. "Damn," he muttered. Refocusing on his goal, he weaved his way around patrons and stood in front of the professor, peering uninhibitedly down her blouse while he waited for her to acknowledge him.

The pretty academic sensed her space had been invaded and looked up from her notes. Immediately aware that his eyes were fixed somewhat lower than hers, she closed her blouse with one hand and smirked disapprovingly. "Can I help you with something," she said shortly.

"My name is Anwar. Can I offer you something...ah... stronger than cola?"

"I don't think so, thank you. I'm not a drinker. I really am rather busy, so if you don't mind..."

"Come now. A young white lady in a foreign land can't have too many friends. Just one drink."

"I think I've made myself clear. No. Thank you. I'm not interested in a drink... nor company."

"As you wish." Abasi bowed slightly and turned, then weaved his way back to the bar. He sat heavily and downed the contents of his glass, enjoying the burn as he gulped. "Unveiled whore," he spit under his breath as he resumed gawking at the source of his rejection. He poured another glass of Changaa. With every sip of his foul drink, his ire rose. With every sip he watched her take through those perfectly pursed lips, his lust increased.

Like blood in the water, the stench of lasciviousness and rage wafted into Hell's chambers, arousing the interest of Cimeries, demon ruler of Africa. He sniffed the acrid air and his nostrils flared to allow for a bigger sampling. He could smell Abasi's lust; his sinuses and throat burned with it; his mouth watered and he began to drool from the corners of his lips. He hurried to mount his phantom horse, a steed as black as the Abyss, and kicked its side, spurring it into motion with the hooked claws on the inside of his scaly legs. In the blink of an eye, Cimeries was at Abasi's side, goading him subliminally into still deeper rapaciousness. "Take the whore, you Allah loving bastard!" Cimeries pressured. "Don't let the white devil treat you like you're a nobody! Who the hell does she think she is! Walking around with no head covering, the little tramp is asking for it." Cimeries' thoughts became Abasi's thoughts as the demon assimilated Abasi's brain.

An uneasy feeling permeated the atmosphere around the table, which caused the young woman to close her notebook, and take a final sip of cola. Without hesitation, she rose from her chair, catching the strap of her knapsack on the arm and flipping the chair onto its back in the process. Purposefully, she walked briskly by Abasi's place at the bar, carefully avoiding eye contact. As she passed, Abasi turned and watched her shapely form as she exited the establishment into the Nairobi night. "Don't let her get away with that!" Cimeries whispered into Abasi's mind. "Take what is owed you. You're a government official, by god! The bitch owes you some respect!"

Anwar Abasi followed his mark into the street, lagging far enough behind to avoid being made. The anthropologist walked briskly, determined to get back to her hotel. She hadn't meant to stay that late in the bar, but she had become so absorbed in her notes that she hadn't noticed the passage of time. Samantha Dunbar, Sam to her friends and close colleagues, was in Kenya studying the rural development of the villages around the capital. As a practicing atheist, she was fascinated by the blending of tribal spiritualism, Catholicism, Anglicanism and Islam on the culture's emergence into a "functioning" 20th Century nation.

Sam was relieved when she stepped across the threshold and into the lobby of her hotel. Bypassing the broken elevator, she entered the dim stairwell and trotted up the two flights to her floor. She fumbled in her knapsack for her room key, found it and hurriedly jammed the key into the lock. Just as she turned the handle, her body slammed into the door, pushing it open with a bang against the wall. The violence of the attack was disorienting. Pinned against the wall, she raked her fingernails across her attackers face, but the result was several retaliatory blows to her face, head and gut. She saw white and sensed she was nearing unconsciousness. Her attacker dragged her helpless body to the bed and began pawing her and tearing at her clothes impatiently.

"Take her!" Cimeries panted. "Take her now!"

Abasi ravaged her. On and on he labored over her, dripping drool and sweat on Samantha's battered body. Cimeries chanted encouragement and laughed as the rape continued. The sheer violence and degradation of it all sent tremors directly into Hell's throne room. Abaddon himself manifested at the unholy union's bedside, not wanting to miss such an opportunity. A surprised Cimeries fell on his face before his master.

"What have we here, Cimeries? An atheist whore and a moon-god worshiper! A veritable orgy of the damned!"

"Yes, my Lord. I was about to summon you."

"You were about to do no such thing, you greedy beggar! You would have kept this all to yourself. Do you think I don't know you by now, demon?" Abaddon laughed.

"You know me all too well, Master," Cimeries grinned. "Forgive my insolence, my Lord."

Not wanting to miss the opportunity, Abaddon entered Abasi's body as the rapist continued to force himself on Samantha. Abasi could hardly feel the master demon's indwelling because of the pervasiveness of his own rancid salaciousness. Abaddon reveled in the lewdness of the moment and the venomous lust streamed through his veins. As Abasi neared the completion of the act, Abaddon took full control and shuddered as he spilled his evil seed into Samantha's helpless body, mixing with Abasi's in an insidious cocktail of sin and death. Samantha's senses could no longer tolerate the attack. As she slipped into blackness, she thought she saw three figures hovering over her, Abasi and two others; their combined weight on her was crushing. She fought to breathe.

"Bravo, Unholy One!" Cimeries offered supportively.

"From this consummation comes the future of the world, Cimeries. Her womb will bear my offspring and he will be ruler over all the earth! To him every knee will bow... My will be done!"

chapter

TWO

I am the Light of the world; he who follows Me will not walk in the darkness, but will have the Light of life.

- John 8:12

NEW COVENANT CHURCH. HOUSTON, TEXAS. THREE YEARS SINCE *THE GATHERING*.

Angelica Proudman went row by row in the empty sanctuary, picking up the service bulletins from the early service and generally straightening things in preparation for the next service. In a church of more than a thousand regular parishioners, there were dozens of volunteers and janitorial staff to accomplish the task, but it was something she enjoyed doing because it was quiet and repetitive, and it gave her time to think, pray and reflect.

"Need some help, Ms. Angie... ummm... Mom?" An energetic Missy Morgan bounced down the aisle toward her mother. Seventeen year old Victoria "Missy" Morgan, now Morgan-Proudman by legal adoption, was just now getting used to calling Angelica "Mom."

"If you're offering," Angelica smiled at her.

"So, I was wondering if you and Dad wanted to take us out for lunch after church?" Missy asked hopefully. "There's a new Mongolian place where you pick your own ingredients and they cook it for you on this enormous wok thingie. Olivia went the other day and she says it is sooo good!"

"Sounds delicious. Let's do it."

"Yay!" Missy said approvingly as she got down on her knees to retrieve a bulletin from under a seat. "Sooo, Matt in the praise band said he would teach me guitar for only $25 a lesson..."

"Sooo, do you know that whenever you say 'sooo' I know you are about to ask for something?" Angelica said with a grin.

"Maybe." Missy chuckled. "I'm sooo predictable, huh?"

"Yes. Yes you are." The two women enjoyed a laugh together. They had become remarkably close, especially since the

Hinnom Valley horror. It seemed so long ago and mostly like a dream during the normal daily routine. Only occasionally now did the memories come as nightmares in the dark hours after midnight, when the house was quiet and the shadows played tricks with their minds.

"I wanted to talk to you privately," Missy said with a more serious tone as their laughter subsided.

"Oh... about?"

"About Israel. About what happened there. About actually seeing the Devil and demons and things that even my Christian friends think I'm crazy when I talk about..."

"I understand. I mean I get it, Missy. Really I do." Angelica tried to reassure her daughter with her most motherly voice. "You've experienced things that most people only imagine. And the reality is more terrifying than anyone could ever fathom."

"That's it exactly. I just want to talk it out with you and Dad. He's so busy though."

"He'll make time for you if you ask him, Missy."

"I know. I just feel... I don't know."

"Would you like me to tell him to set some time aside for you?"

"Maybe that would get the conversation started," Missy agreed.

"Ok. After the last service... I'll pin him down and sit on him if necessary!"

"That'll work." Missy felt better already. She trusted that Angelica would not rest until she had gotten the three of them together to talk. It wasn't as if the experience had debilitated her these past three years. In her estimation she had dealt with it quite well. Her faith and new life in Christ had delivered on its promise to give her a hope and a future. Still, the kidnapping, psychological torture and spiritual attacks on her person and on her friend, Olivia, had taken a toll on her. Since then, she no longer had a sense of innocence. Gone were any child-like notions and fantasies. The supernatural reality of evil incarnate obliterated such sentimentalities entirely. She had seen it, touched it, and experienced it ALL. The monsters under her childhood bed had turned out to be real, and processing that reality was hard. There was nothing left to the imagination of her youth.

NAIROBI, KENYA. MAY 1961.

An obviously pregnant Samantha Dunbar paced nervously in front of the State House, trying to decide if going inside was the best course of action. She'd worked out the details in her head and rehearsed over and over the way she thought the confrontation would go, but now that she was here, outside his office at the

Ministry of Finance, she found her resolve waning. But then she thought of the alternative. There was no way she could continue as she was. For the past five months she had been able to keep her embarrassing condition under wraps. The university had no idea she was with child, but she was due to return stateside soon. What would her colleagues say? Surely her department would fire her – an unwed professor, pregnant! Scandalous!

When she first realized her predicament, she had sought a permanent solution. But the memories of that horror nearly made her lose her mind. Through some of the local village spiritualists she had met in her research, she learned of a practitioner that dabbled in the dark arts and in troublesome pregnancies. Her visit to his place of business proved much more than she could have ever imagined. The "clinic" was housed in a small corrugated tin shack on the outskirts of the village of Nyang'oma Kogelo, in the Nyanza Province. Upon entering the shack, Sam was greeted by a shirtless, elderly, Luo tribesman in tattered trousers. He motioned for Sam to lie back on a straw mat, which she did reluctantly. He looked her over and touched her lightly and poked her intermittently as she explained what she needed. As she spoke, the practitioner moved his trembling hands over her body, and then abruptly broke into her personal space, sniffing at her in long drawn-out sniffs. His nostrils twitched as he smelled her, and as his face passed over her belly, he paused and inhaled deeply. "Shetani," he whispered, fear evident in his trembling voice. He backed away slowly. "Shetani." His whisper became a terrified whimper as he reached for a crude straw broom and pushed at Sam with it forcefully. "Shetani!"

"Stop that!" Sam scooted off the mat and away from the broom. "What's with you? What's 'Shetani?'"

"Shetani! Demon in your belly!"

Sam managed to pull herself to her feet and ran out of the shack, leaving the crazed witch doctor to his ranting. "Shetani!" he shouted after her.

The memory confused and haunted her. One thing was certain in Sam's mind because of the unsettling experience: Abortion was not the solution. She would have the child, but she would make sure that her future was secure in the process. Her mind made up, she marched with intensity through the State House doors.

PRESENT DAY.

The morning storm was lingering and Proudman found himself back at his office window watching the rain once again. Proudman sensed that there was something foreboding in it, although he couldn't discern anything specific. As the hour of the second Sunday service approached, the preacher gathered his sermon notes for a second run at the congregation. He entered the sanctuary and took a seat next to Angelica, who squeezed his hand and smiled at him with a look that said, "Knock 'em dead!"

The band's worship set wrapped up and the keyboardist played long, soulful notes as Proudman mounted the platform for the second time that morning. He spread out his sermon notes as before, and was about to launch into the same sermon as in the first service, just as he'd always done, when he suddenly felt a fire ignite in his belly. His body tingled as if electricity were passing through it. The Holy Spirit pulled at him with such force that he simply bowed his head in submission and began to pray out loud.

"Father, God, I don't know where You're about to take us, but I am Your obedient servant. Lead on Holy Spirit." Proudman looked around the immense sanctuary at the many faces, expectantly looking back at him. "Normally, if you were to sit through both services on any given Sunday, you would hear the same message, with only minor deviations as the Holy Spirit leads. But this morning, the message you're about to hear is going to be completely different from the one I gave in the early service. I can see from here that my lovely wife is somewhat relieved!" Muffled laughter rose from the crowd of nearly six hundred strong. "I have no idea what this sermon will be about, so when I reach the end, it will be as much of a surprise to me as it is to you... so let's get started!"

Proudman paused for a moment and closed his eyes. Anticipation grew in the congregation and Proudman could sense the minute or two of uncomfortable silence, but he would not rush the Holy Spirit. Finally, he began, "When we think of Jesus Christ, we usually tend to think of the books of the Bible that chronicle His birth, His ministry and His death and resurrection. Then, perhaps, we might think of His disciples, carrying His Word throughout the remainder of the New Testament; or of the Apostle Paul writing to the early Church, and laying out for us the systematic theology we enjoy today. I'm here today to tell you about the Christ in terms that are less frequently discussed, but just as real, just as valid, just as important to understanding your faith, as the Christ of the New Testament. I'm here today to talk with you about the Christ of the Old Testament... the Christ at the beginning of the Book... the Christ of Genesis.

You may be thinking, 'Jesus in Genesis? I've read Genesis, and Preacher, Jesus Christ is not in it!' On the surface it might appear that way, but let's look a little deeper. What is the opening chapter of Genesis about? Anyone?" Proudman walked the length of the platform and pointed to people as they vocalized their answers.

"Yes! The opening chapter of Genesis is about creation. The first statement says it all, *'In the beginning God created the heaven and the earth.'* The story, OUR story, begins with God, the Creator... the all-powerful God, who, out of nothing, created something by the sheer force of His will and with the power of His spoken word. Perfect God created a perfect heaven and a perfect earth. The world began with God. All... things... be-gin... with God." Proudman paused to assess his audience. The silence was interrupted only by the random cough or soft rustle of paper as parishioners took notes.

"In the six days that followed, God transformed the heavens and the earth, making them into works of His perfect will. God created order out of the nothingness and when all was done, God proclaimed His creation, including mankind, 'very good.' What is particularly interesting is that God's creation, or perhaps more accurately, the activity of His creating, was not done there. The fact is, God is still creating today!" Proudman smiled and walked the platform again, acknowledging the puzzled faces.

"'What?' You say!" Proudman voiced what many were thinking.

"Yes! God is still actively creating, even today, this very morning! 2 Corinthians 5:17 says, *'If anyone is in Christ, he is a new creation...'* Each one of us, as we accept Christ, undergoes a transformation, a re-generation, a genesis experience where we become newly created, and we become just as mankind was in the beginning... the perfect, image and likeness of God. Isn't that amazing?

The next couple of verses in Genesis 1 paint a picture of the transformation process each of us goes through as we are saved. Let me explain: Verse 2 says, *'The earth was formless and void, and darkness was over the surface of the deep, and the Spirit of God was moving over the surface of the waters.'*

Each of us, before we are touched by the saving grace of God are formless and void. We are empty vessels, walking the earth in search of satisfaction, and attempting to fill the void with all manner of things: careers, hobbies, relationships, and what-not. And as those things fail to adequately fill the emptiness in our being, some of us resign ourselves to the mediocrity of the unfulfilled, convincing ourselves that this is as good as it gets. And then, some of us try more desperate means of filling the void by immersing ourselves in relentless pursuits for money, status, power, possessions, and the like. And, when those things fail to satisfy, some of us escalate our behaviors into alcohol and substance abuse, unhealthy relationships and self-destructive activities. Our lives are without structure. We are formless and void and living in the darkness, over-our-heads in the deep water..." Proudman's voice rose to a thunderous crescendo.

Then, in stark contrast, he whispered, "But, the Holy Spirit of God is there... He is there moving over the surface of the water... the very water in which we are treading like mad to stay afloat. And just as we are going under for the last time; as our heads are hopelessly covered by the dark, deep water, we reach up our hands and cry out, 'Abba, Father! Save me!' And that's when it happens... Verses 3 and 4 say:

'Then God said, "Let there be light; and there was light." God saw that the light was good; and God separated the light from the darkness.' The Holy Spirit reaches down into the deep, dark water and grabs us by the hand and by the heart and points us to the light. The Spirit shows us the light and the light is Jesus Christ! In John 8:12, Jesus says, *'I am the Light of the world; he who follows Me will not walk in the darkness, but will have the Light of life.'* As we accept Christ, we too become light, we are the light of the world, and God sees us, and when he does He sees that we are now <u>good</u>! We are now, through the light of Christ, <u>acceptable</u> to God the Father. When we decide to follow Jesus, we no longer walk in darkness, but we have the light of eternal life within us. We are separated, once and for all, from the darkness of our former, hopeless existence! We say that we are saved."

Proudman walked to the podium and poured himself a glass of water from a pitcher staged on a small round table. He took a long pull on the glass and continued in a slow, deliberate tone, "Salvation is Christ-centered. To be saved, one must be in Christ, or perhaps more simply, one must have a relationship of acceptance of Christ as Savior. But, realize the story of salvation did not begin in the manger. 1 Peter 1:20-21 says, *For He [Christ] was foreknown before the foundation of the world, but has appeared in these last times for the sake of you, who through Him, are believers in God, who raised Him from the dead and gave Him glory, so that your faith and hope are in God.'*

The word 'foreknown' from the original translation means 'actively involved in,' which tells us in no uncertain terms that Christ was not just present *for*, but rather was an active participant *in* the creation of the world. Christ was the architect of the Plan for the universe, including our world... and our salvation. He is the author and perfecter of our faith.

As a new creation in Christ, the sinner is saved by grace, and, through the act of repentance, believes on Christ..." Proudman paused thoughtfully and then explained, "As a side note: Does everyone understand the significance of the phrase *'believe on'* versus *'believe in?'* To believe *in* something is simply to acknowledge its existence. To believe *on* something is to completely base your life on its principles, values and worth. It is your absolute Truth. So to complete that thought, as I was saying, as a new creation in Christ, the sinner is saved by grace, and, through the act of repentance, believes on Christ, and approaches the throne of God blameless. And, as in all things, the salvation process began with God. Ephesians 1:4 tells us that, *'He [God] chose us in Him [Christ] before the foundation of the world, that we would be holy and blameless before Him [God] in love.'*

So, to understand this correctly, let's pause here for a moment. Before God created the world, before the sixth day, when He created man, He knew that we would be tempted and fall out of grace by sin. God knew that we would mess things up, even before He formed us into being. Our sin did not take God by surprise. In fact He had a plan to deal with it even before it occurred! As the scripture says, *'He chose us in Christ before the foundation of the world, that we would be holy and blameless before Him in love.'*

Ephesians 1:5 says that we were *'predestined to be His children through Jesus Christ to Himself, according to the kind intention of His will.'* Think for a moment what that means in terms of the creation story. Each of us was chosen by our Creator before the world was made, to be reconciled out of the bondage of sin by Jesus Christ, so that we could be with the Father, because He loves us and wants us to be near Him."

Proudman sensed a murmur of uneasiness and paused immediately to address it. "I want to make sure that this word, 'predestined,' does not trip anyone up. It simply means this:

+ God determined beforehand that anyone who believes on Christ will become His child and be one with Christ

+ The choice we make begins with God... God chooses us first!

+ He does it out of love for us; it is a free gift available to all who would believe on Christ

+ It is based on the good pleasure of His perfect will

+ Its purpose is to glorify God

+ It does not relieve us of our responsibility to believe on Christ in order to personally bring to pass God's predestination

+ Our ability to believe occurs through the power of the Holy Spirit, who was also present with God the Father and Christ the Son before the foundation of the world

I hope that's clear to everyone, but if you only take one thing away from this part... remember this: We have the responsibility to believe on Christ to fully engage in the salvation process... it does not occur without our fulfilling our end of the deal, which is to believe on Him – to repent of sin – to turn away from sin – and turn toward Christ!"

Proudman paced the platform looking for signs from his church that everyone was ready to move on.

"When I deliver a message, I always like to ask the question, 'Why is this relevant today?' Friends, the world outside these New Covenant Church walls is a crazy place. I don't have to tell you that people are struggling and in fear for their day to day existence. In the natural world, there is chaos. If you turned on the TV this morning as you were getting ready to come here, there was in all probability last night a robbery or a murder, a home invasion or a fire that ripped apart yet another family in the area. I don't have to tell you that, this morning, in this very city, there are families struggling with the loss of their precious loved ones.

As you got dressed, you might have said a little prayer for the devastated families on the news, and perhaps a prayer of thanksgiving that it wasn't you or your family. That's ok. I know I've done it: Thanking God silently that, by His grace and mercy, while you and your family slept, the evils of the dark night passed you by and left you in peace to wake safe and sound in your bed. Sometimes it seems that there is just no hope for things to get better. In fact every indication in the world shows that things might get worse. But that's the world-view. But, that's if it depended solely on our own ability to fix things. The good news is that it doesn't depend on us... the good news is that there is a Plan... a Plan that was put into motion before the fall of Lucifer and the angels, before the fall of Adam and Eve in the Garden, before you took your first breath of air on this earth!" The preacher stopped and surveyed the auditorium. He could perceive a sense of affirmation that the congregation was indeed receiving what he was saying. Proudman knew with certainty that this lesson on Christ in creation was not of his own doing. Why he was being led here, only God knew.

"Here's the point, church: The gift of your salvation was not an afterthought. God didn't sit stewing in heaven about how man had screwed things up and then decide that His only option to get His wayward children back was to go to Plan 'B.' And, Plan 'B' was not when God the Father went to God the Son and said, "Well, I guess somebody's gonna have to clean this mess up and pay for all the damages..." God didn't mess up when He created us and then have to re-think everything He had created! God is not in heaven second guessing Himself! God is a God of second chances, not a God of second guesses!"

The statement resonated with many as several voices in the congregation spoke out: "Amen!

"Preach it!"

Proudman took advantage of the response to take another sip of water. He was amazed at the strength of the message and the clarity of thought possessing him. He had preached salvation sermons before, but not like this one. "His plan for our salvation is not the result of His miscalculation during the creation process. It was the plan all along, from the very foundation of the world. The Bible says in 1 John 4:19, *'We love, because He first loved us.'* God loved us in the beginning. So he chose us. We, by choosing Christ as our Savior, love Him in return. That is the redemptive process of salvation in its purest form.

Our God is omniscient. He is all-knowing. It is His character. God knew before the foundation of the world... God knew before He created us that this is the way it would go. We would fall, we would die, we would be separated from Him, we would spend our eternity apart from Him in hell except... except if we chose Christ as our Savior. God the Father, God the Son and God the Holy Spirit – three persons, one God – laid out the plan in the beginning, before everything was made.

What a magnificent plan! Not Plan 'B!' No people, this was Plan 'A' all along! This was THE Plan. From the time God created the heaven and the earth, to the time He created mankind, to the time mankind sinned against Him and fell from grace, to the time God sent the Son to pay for our sins with His death on the cross, to the time when each of us individually chose Christ to redeem us and bring us back to the Father... that was the Plan all along! God wants us... to want Him." Proudman chuckled. "There's a song in there somewhere." The congregation laughed in appreciation of the 1975 Cheap Trick reference. "The obscure song references are included in your price of admission, people. But back to the message...What's more, God wants us to use our free will to get to Him. We are not angels, who know Him in fact. We are humans who know Him in Faith! Angels can see Him every day, and so they worship Him. Humans choose to love Him based purely on Faith that He exists, and worship Him in Faith without seeing Him. That's a tremendous thing, church! What a gift! What a Plan!"

Proudman stopped as the last thought reverberated around the church. He waited long enough for the spontaneous clapping to subside and then began again in a controlled tone. "So where do we go from here? What do we do with this information now that we have it? I don't want to send you out from here today without something useful to take with you into the rest of your week. I don't want to send you into the world without asking the Holy Spirit to move in this place and meet each of you where you are now in your individual faith journey... and then to encourage you to take a step further... to take a step out of your comfort zone and ask Him to enter your circumstances and heal something specific that needs His touch. There may be health concerns, there may be fear of the unknown, there may be broken relationships, there may be financial problems, there may be problems at work...whatever the situation, God knows what you need and the Holy Spirit was sent for times like these, for your comfort... in fact He is the Holy Comforter, the descending Dove of peace that passes all understanding... invite Him in and allow Him to work on your behalf...

And, I want you to be encouraged as you gaze expectantly into the distance of your future; because the God who planned for your redemption also planned for your future to be good and prosperous. *'For I know the plans I have for you,' declares the Lord, 'plans to prosper you and not to harm you, plans to give you hope and a future.'* –that's Jeremiah 29:11. Take that scripture with you this week and let it encourage you. And as you are encouraged, be also challenged by this thought from Hebrews 12:1-3:

'Therefore, since we have so great a cloud of witnesses surrounding us, let us also lay aside every encumbrance and the sin which so easily entangles us, and let us run with endurance the race that is set before us, fixing our eyes on Jesus, the author and perfecter of faith, who for the joy set before Him endured the cross, despising the shame, and has sat down at the right hand of the throne of God. For consider Him who has endured such hostility by sinners against Himself, so that you will not grow weary and lose heart.'

The challenge is to let Jesus be your example, so that you can be an example to others. As Christians, know that you are being watched by seekers everywhere you go. When a seeker looks at you, do they want what you have? Do they recognize that your life is every bit as hard as theirs, but that you seem to rise above the fray and shine regardless of the circumstances? Are you running your race with endurance, empowered by the presence of the Holy Spirit in your life? Do they want what you have? And if they do, are you willing to share it so that they can have it too?

Pray with me. Father God, Creator of the Universe, Maker of all things, seen and unseen... We give You praise! We give You honor and glory for the perfect Plan You set into motion before the foundations of the world. Before anything was made, Father, before You spoke the Word and out of nothing You caused the heavens and the earth into being... before any of that You knew how our salvation would be accomplished We give You all the glory Father, Son and Holy Spirit... that Your perfect Plan remains in motion, as it was, is and will always be, to bring Your children back to You as blameless and as spotless as You created us to be. Our prayer this morning, Father, is that we remember You always by running our race with endurance and by loving You because You first loved us. We pray all of this in the name of the One who was there in the beginning, with You and the Holy Spirit ...the One who is the author and perfecter of our faith, our Redeemer, Jesus Christ. Amen."

As Proudman finished his prayer, the praise team began to play a worshipful melody and the spent preacher dismounted the platform and allowed the worship leader to take the church. Angelica stood holding his arm. Proudman looked at his family there on the front row and gave thanks to God that each of them already had the essential relationship with Christ he had just presented. "Thank you, Father, for loving them," he prayed silently.

NAIROBI, KENYA. MAY 1961.

Samantha Dunbar walked intently across the State House lobby to the receptionist. "Samantha Dunbar to see Anwar Abasi," she stated succinctly.

"Do you have an appointment, Madame? I don't see you on his schedule today."

"Appointment? No. But please tell him I am here and that the matter is urgent. I must speak with him now!"

"Very well, Madame. Please have a seat while I try his assistant." The receptionist reached for the clunky, black phone and dialed the switchboard, tapping her pencil impatiently as she waited to be connected.

Sam surveyed her surroundings. The lobby was appointed in heavy wood furnishings of English influence. The government building was bustling with people carrying papers and waiting in lines outside various offices. It wasn't but a few months ago that Sam stood in one of those lines, waiting to have her visa authorized so she could remain in Kenya to complete her research. It seemed so long ago, given her current circumstances, as if it happened to a different Samantha. She ran over once again in her mind what she would say and practiced her "I-mean-business look" in her compact mirror as she checked her makeup. As she rehearsed, a young Kenyan woman emerged over the top of Sam's compact mirror. Sam looked up and smiled slightly.

"Mr. Abasi will see you now."

Sam nodded and stood. She felt as if her legs would give way at any moment and the walk back to Abasi's office was as close to an out-of-body experience as Sam had ever had. Abasi's office was less than stately. It was small and dark with a small window randomly placed near the ceiling on one wall. His utilitarian desk was cluttered with stacks of papers, and he sat behind it, looking rather small and insignificant with his round-lensed eyeglasses perched on the end of his dark, broad nose. If Abasi was surprised to see Sam, especially in her current condition, he didn't show it.

"What do you want?" he asked pointedly.

"Just one thing from you," Sam replied just as sternly.

"And what might that be?" Abasi removed his glasses from the tip of his nose and glared into Sam's eyes. Sam noticed that his eyes were empty and soulless, and they were yellowed and bloodshot.

"Let's get the facts on the table," Sam took control of the conversation. "You raped me. You took my dignity and you left me with nothing but this child inside me and with no hope for a future career or means of taking care of it."

"Why are you keeping it?" Abasi asked heartlessly.

"Oh, I tried to be rid of it, believe me. No one will touch it. It's as if they can sense that it came from your foul, disgusting act and for some reason they are afraid of it."

"Ridiculous!"

"That may be, but it's true nonetheless. So, to my point... I don't want your money or your time or anything to do with you except... except I want you to give this child your name." Sam put her practiced "look" into play.

"My name? Out of the question. I will not put my reputation on the line for you or the little bastard you carry. And, for the record, not that it matters; nobody raped you. Your words said 'no' but your actions said 'yes.'"

Sam strained to control her anger and to stay on task. She refused to let him get under her skin. "I was afraid you might respond this way, so I've taken steps."

"Steps?"

"Yes. Steps." Sam continued the glare. "I've taken the time to write down the events of the night you raped me." Sam placed special emphasis on the words, *'you raped me.'* "I have statements from the hotel manager swearing to your uninvited presence at my hotel that night, and from the bar keeper swearing to your failed attempts to pick me up at his establishment, and testimony supporting the fact that you followed me out of the bar. All of this I have placed with a friend here in Nairobi who will hand-deliver them to the Minister of Finance, your boss, once I depart Kenya or if anything were to happen to me." Sam paused long enough to see if she had made an impact. Clearly she had. Beads of sweat formed on Abasi's forehead. "All you have to do to prevent that from occurring is sign the papers at the hospital as the baby's father so that you will be on the birth certificate. I will return to the United States with the child and you will never hear from me again."

Abasi looked at Sam, studying her. "Agreed," he said after a long silence. "But, I want the evidence documents once the birth certificate is done."

"Agreed, with one stipulation... you will only get them once I am safely out of the country."

"Agreed. Very well, then. Please show yourself out. I'm very busy."

Samantha Dunbar left the dingy office quickly. Her gait increased and she did not slow until she was outside the State House, where she leaned heavily on a column for a moment to catch her breath. In less than three months, the baby would arrive and she would depart for home. Until then, she would stay out of sight as much as possible for fear of retaliation from Abasi.

HELL. THREE YEARS SINCE *THE GATHERING.*

Abaddon gathered himself and pushed his delicious depression into the blackness of his soulless core. No time to wallow in his misery now that the child had grown to manhood and was poised on the edge of the precipice of eternal greatness. It was time the spawn of Satan knew his identity and purpose.

Several demons entered the chamber with a selection of business suits, shoes and accessories. They laid them in front of Abaddon and waited silently as he perused them, gliding his black fingernails over the expensive fabric. He liked dressing up in the styles of men. For centuries he had often visited the world dressed in the finest offerings of the period. He had always, from the time of their creation, envied mankind. They were fragile and easily manipulated, but they had great passion and God loved them all so completely – even the ones that disobeyed Him and turned from Him. "Why didn't God love the angels in that same way?" he'd often wondered. His jealousy turned to hate, and his hate to the venomous rage that presently consumed him. But he had a plan. A seed injected into the fertile womb of a non-believer had grown to the fullness of manhood. The child had been carefully tended to, attending the finest schools, meeting the right connections, who dutifully carried out Satan's will by any means necessary, eliminating any and all barriers impeding his rise to political power.

Abaddon materialized in an office in the Hart Office Building on Capitol Hill, a place he knew like the back of his hand. The building was quiet as the earth-hour was early yet. The senator from Illinois, Anwar Abasi, Jr., had not yet arrived for work. Abaddon scanned the office, which was cleanly furnished, neat and organized. On a credenza lay an open guitar case with a Gibson Les Paul guitar adorned with a "Rock The Vote" logo. Centered at one end of the room was Abasi's desk, its highly polished surface devoid of papers, with framed photographs of his family on one corner and a copy of his first book on the other. In front of the desk, angled precisely, were two chairs for visitors, nicely upholstered with stately blue fabric. Behind the desk sat the obligatory high-backed, leather power-chair, which was elevated slightly higher than the visitors' chairs. Opposite the desk, were two brown leather chairs in a separate sitting area, and between them an African table inlaid with tribal designs and the words "Senator Anwar Abasi USA" in a circular pattern in the center. Adjacent to the desk was another credenza holding framed photographs and decorative presentation boxes opened to reveal commemorative coins. Above the credenza, a portrait of the late U.S. Supreme Court Justice Thurgood Marshall and just to the left of it, above the light switches, a photo of the Hawaiian cliff where Anwar had scattered into the winds and Pacific waves, his dear mother, Samantha's, ashes. The remainder of the room was unremarkable, except for a carved wooden hand holding an egg, a campaign gift from Kenya, symbolizing the fragility of life; and a painting by Senator Ted Kennedy dedicated to Abasi with the words, "To Anwar – I love your audacity. With great respect and warmest wishes."

Abaddon sat in the high-backed desk chair and closed his eyes to await his son, the senator. He rubbed his forehead with long, pasty fingers, ignoring as best he could, the raised, cross-shaped scar tissue as he did so.

NEW COVENANT CHURCH. HOUSTON, TEXAS.

No sooner had the worship band played their last note on the closing song and Missy Morgan-Proudman was right on Angelica's heels as they left the sanctuary and headed back to Pastor Geoffrey Proudman's office behind the platform. "We have to get to him before someone else does or we'll never get to talk to him and we'll never get to the Mongolian place for lunch," Angelica said as they trotted down the hallway.

"I saw several people eyeballing him to see which way he was going, so hurry!" Missy laughed through her words.

As the two Proudman ladies approached the Pastor's office, they saw one of the church vestry members, Jim Clancy, walking that way ahead of them. Quickly slipping by him on both sides, Missy and Angelica reached the door handle just as the surprised man was about to extend a hand to it. "Sorry, this can't wait," Missy said as she backed through the door.

"Family matter... very important. Thanks for your under-standing." Angelica smiled apologetically and backed through the door behind Missy, closing it in the befuddled man's face as he tried in vain to protest.

Geoffrey Proudman looked up from his desk at the sud-den appearance of his lovely wife and daughter. "Was that Jim Clancy I saw at the door?"

"I... umm... not sure," Missy offered.

"What are you two up to?" Proudman could see that some-thing was afoot.

"Your daughter needs our undivided attention for a few minutes and then we want you to take us to lunch at the new Mongolian place. And, we aren't taking 'no' or 'not now' as pos-sible answers." Angelica knew how to get Geoffrey's attention.

"So don't you even worry about Jim, or whoever else...They can wait!" Missy added.

"Okay. You have my undivided attention!" Proudman smiled. "These girls are so much alike," he thought to him-self. "If I didn't know better, I'd swear they were blood-relat-ed."

Angelica nodded at Missy, encouraging her to speak. Missy Morgan adjusted her position on the couch and then adjusted her skirt as she crossed her legs uncomfortably. She then played thoughtfully with her watch, kicked off her shoes and finally settled on sitting cross-legged before she began speaking. "I've been dealing with some stuff..." As she slowly chose her words, she stared intently at the ankle bracelet she wore, fiddling with the delicately dangling cross charm, the same one she and Olivia wore during the ordeal in the Hinnom Valley. "...stuff about what we went through in Israel."

"What kind of stuff, sweetheart?" Proudman's patience and concern were evident in his tone. It had been a while since anyone had brought up the ordeal, but he sensed that it was always right below the surface. He knew it was for him, so he could only assume it was the same for all concerned.

"It just seems as if... oh I don't know... it just seems like it's not over." Missy struggled to articulate the feelings of dread and impending doom she had been experiencing. "I mean, I know we sent Satan back to hell, but there is this... feeling. And I keep having nightmares about that thing that nearly killed Olivia in the dungeon at the old monastery. It's like it's watching me, waiting for an opportunity to attack."

"I understand," Proudman nodded. "Just this morning I was looking at the storm clouds outside my window and I got the distinct sense that something was coming. Something destructive and terrible."

"So it's not just Angelica and me?" Missy asked.

"You're feeling it too?" Geoffrey looked at his wife.

"Yes." Angelica responded intently.

"Then we should probably get in touch with Simon and Rachel in Jerusalem to see if they are getting the same message. And Jordan... And Moishe, of course. I'll call them this afternoon. I'm not sure if this is anything more than post-traumatic stress, but it won't hurt to dig a little deeper just to be sure. In the meantime, let's try and keep our heads and keep things as normal as possible around here... agreed?"

"And just how do we do that?" Missy asked with a less-than-satisfied tone.

"Lunch at the new Mongolian place sounds like a great way to start," Proudman offered hopefully. "Look, Missy, I'm going to look into this, I promise. I am taking your feelings seriously, especially since we all seem to be having similar thoughts. Okay?"

"Okay." Missy conceded. Mongolian did sound good to her. And, it was her idea after all. "Gotta eat," she admitted with a half-hearted smile.

"Great!" Go round up your three brothers and let's go before good ol' Jim comes knocking again!"

"Meet you by the car." Missy bounced off the couch and into her shoes and was out the door in one smooth motion.

"Are you worried?" Angelica asked frankly.

"I am. The feelings are too constant and oppressive to be just PTSD. And the fact that we are all in tune to them is... "

"It's frightening," Angelica completed his thought.

HART SENATE OFFICE BUILDING. WASHINGTON, D.C.

Senator Anwar Muhammad Abasi, Jr. arrived at his office just past 8:30 a.m. dressed in his best golfing attire. He intended to make a few calls and then head out to the golf course for eighteen holes with a couple of campaign supporters before a fundraising event later that evening. He loved golf. He loved leisure time in general. And he loved campaigning. In fact campaigning was the part of politics he liked best of all – it was his forte'. He always made it a point to tell people that he got in to politics to help the poor and struggling middle class American get a fair shake. He had rehearsed the line so often that part of him actually had begun to believe it. The truth was that Anwar Abasi didn't care about the poor or middle class at all. He preferred hobnobbing with the Hollywood elite and with sports and music celebrities.

Something about their shallowness and lack of sincerity resonated with him. When he looked at himself... really analyzed himself... they were the type with whom he most identified.

Abasi greeted his assistant with the obligatory nod and a polite, "Good morning," as he eased by her desk and through the door to his inner office before she could give him the usual stack of annoying phone messages. "No time for those," he thought to himself. "Too much like actual work, and there's golf to be played," he muttered under his breath.

The office seemed a bit chillier than usual to Abasi as he flipped on the panel of light switches just inside the door. His eyes went immediately to the thermostat on an adjacent wall and he walked briskly toward it without noticing Abaddon seated behind his desk. "Fifty-two degrees?" he said in disbelief. The thermostat was set at 74 degrees, but the thermometer read much lower. "Must be broken," he said out loud.

"No. It works just fine." Abaddon spoke up.

Abasi stepped backward as his brain registered the source of the voice that had jarred his consciousness. He sucked in a breath and every muscle tensed as his flight instinct kicked in. He wanted to run, but his body failed to respond correctly to the urge. His synapses misfired and he collapsed jerkily into a heap on his office floor. Realizing he had not succeeded in a successful retreat, Abasi began kicking backward, scooting on his backside away from the desk from where he understood the voice to be coming.

Abaddon rose from the high-backed leather chair and looked down disgustedly at his cowardly son flailing like a catfish on the carpet. "Are you kidding me?" Abaddon said with displeasure ringing in his voice.

"Who are you?" Abasi trembled.

"I am... well, you know deep down who I am, Anwar."

"I don't know you... Please don't kill me."

"Kill you?" Abaddon smirked. "That would be extremely... counter-productive."

"What do you want?"

"Wrong question. More to the point, I think, is what do YOU want?"

"What do I want?"

"Yes, Anwar. What do you want?" Abaddon walked around the desk and extended a cold hand to his son. Abasi hesitated. "Come now, Anwar. Man up. Grow a set!" Abasi extended his hand cautiously and Abaddon grasped it firmly and pulled him to his feet in a swift motion, causing him to come eye to eye with his intruder. Abaddon breathed heavily into Abasi's face as his eyes penetrated deeply into Abasi's conflicted soul. "Back to the question at hand... What do you want, Anwar?" Abaddon said breathily.

"I... don't... know..." Abasi struggled for an answer.

"Yes you do! You've always known. It's deep within you, Anwar! Ask for it, and I will give it to you... just as I have, for all these years, given you dreams of greatness! Think, my son, about the dreams you've had... dreams from your father!"

"Dreams... from my father," Abasi repeated blankly. "My father's in Kenya... dead and buried."

"Is he? I think you know the truth, Anwar. The man whose name you bear could never provide you with the things I have given you. From the time you were just a boy I made certain that you attended only the best schools. I provided you with people who would nurture you, care for you, and teach you the ways of the world. I chose your mother because I knew I could count on her secular humanism to keep you out of the clutches of those dreadful Christ-followers. And I knew that you would come to embrace the brotherhood of Islam because, deep down in your soul, you would recognize it as a gateway to a real relationship with me. My son... all that you are is the result of my careful manipulation. You can't help but be who you are and you can't help but want the same things that I want. So tell me... what is it you want?"

"I want... I want..." he stuttered.

"Say it!"

"I want... POWER!"

"YES! And more than power, my son... You, like me, want to be worshipped by all mankind!" Abaddon's black eyes glazed over as the intoxicating thought of people bowing down to him overcame him.

"Worshipped. Yes." Anwar's eyes became mirrors of his father's.

The Proudman family settled in to the table at the new Mongolian restaurant down the street from New Covenant Church. Geoffrey Proudman looked around the table and could hardly believe how blessed he was. Seated on his right, smiling and laughing with her children, was his beloved Angelica. Proudman knew she was in his life because God had ordained it to be so. Next to Angelica sat her son, now their son, Freddie. A strapping young lad with a sharp mind for math and a body made for cross country running. Proudman was pleased with Freddie's future prospects because of his ability to win academic and athletic scholarships, but more than that, Proudman was pleased with his love for Jesus and his steadfast moral character.

Next to Freddie was his partner in crime, Victoria "Missy" Morgan-Proudman. The two were close in age and opposites in disposition, which somehow made them inseparable. Geoffrey had first met Missy at their campsite at *The Gathering* in Israel and was immediately taken with her spiritual maturity. He and Angelica had adopted her into the Proudman family along with her older brothers, Christian Peter (C.P.) and Alexander Morgan-Proudman. Alex, the oldest, was now 21 and had recently enlisted in the Marine Reserves. His unit was due to deploy to Afghanistan in a matter of weeks.

C.P. was 19 and attending Stephen F. Austin University as a physics major and an Army ROTC soldier. C.P. wanted to fly helicopters and eventually jet aircraft. He was a frequent flyer on the university's dean's list and, as a college sophomore, was already exceling academically despite a rough high-school career. Things were really taking off for him, and his love life was looking up too since meeting his girlfriend, Hannah. Proudman thought Hannah was a good complement to C.P.'s character. She was a godly young woman who insisted on church attendance, praying together and putting Jesus in the center of their developing relationship. Just what C.P. needed in Proudman's estimation... a moral compass and, eventually perhaps, a Proverbs 31 helpmate.

Proudman could not be more proud of his children and he was ever aware that the opportunities to have all of them gathered around the same table like this were becoming, more and more, rare occurrences.

chapter

THREE

But since we are of the day, let us be sober, having put on the breastplate of faith and love, and as a helmet, the hope of salvation.

-1 Thessalonians 5:8

CAMPAIGN HEADQUARTERS OF PRESIDENT-ELECT ANWAR MUHAMMAD ABASI, JR. WASHINGTON, D.C. PRESENT DAY. FOUR YEARS SINCE *THE GATHERING.*

Abasi stared at the mess strewn about his campaign headquarters. Mounds of red, white and blue confetti and streamers covered everything. Cheap, plastic stemware dotted the work tables and computer desks, some with flat champagne still in them or puddled around them. Banners around the room trumpeted his name, "Anwar Abasi for President." Abasi soaked it all in. It had been just shy of one year ago that Abaddon had appeared in his office in the Hart Senate Building. He reflected on his confessed desire for power during that first encounter with his father, Satan, and now he was just a few weeks away from being inaugurated as the next President of the United States.

His rise to power had been swift and carefully orchestrated. Abaddon had seen to it that legions of demons had permeated the media, manipulating its people at all levels, from the frontline reporters to the heads of communication conglomerates. Not that the demons were necessary in that arena; for the most part the media people were ready to buy in to the progressive rhetoric shoveled out by the Abasi Campaign. The demons were more of an insurance policy, and their efforts were concentrated on establishing an atmosphere of continuous deception throughout the campaign, with their influence squashing any pangs of conscience that might surface in media personnel as they morphed from professional news people into propaganda peddlers for the new world order.

Where the demonic legions were most effective was in their attack on the high concentrations of urban dwellers in the inner cities. In these densely populated areas, scores of demons were able to intensify the attitude of entitlement inherent in the culture and turn normally politically apathetic people in to pro-Abasi zealots. Using race-baiters and activists, such as Al Sharpton and Jessie Jackson, the demons were able to mobilize a massive voting bloc of thugs, crack heads and welfare queens, bought with the promise of free cell-phones, free housing and food stamps.

Abasi was coming to grips with his identity. At times it was a bit overwhelming, and he wrestled with it. But mostly he bathed in the euphoric knowledge that he was the son of Satan. Abasi closed his eyes and thought about conversing with his father. Immediately Abaddon materialized next to him. The suddenness of Satan's appearance startled Abasi, and Abaddon chuckled and shook his head as he spoke. "We're going to have to toughen you up. You're as skittish as they come."

"Just wasn't expecting you to respond to my thoughts is all."

"Your thoughts are my thoughts, my son."

"So, where do we go from here?"

Abaddon strolled casually over to a campaign banner and ran his black nail over the edge of it. "You promised them hope and change... let's give them the illusion of the former and plenty of the latter."

"What does that mean, exactly?"

"After the inauguration ceremony, we will discuss the details. For now, go enjoy the spoils of your victory; take that presidential title out for a spin and see what it can do; shake some hands, eat some babies..."

"Kiss."

"Come again?"

"Kiss some babies. You said, 'eat some babies.' You meant to say kiss..."

"Did I?" Abaddon laughed loudly as he vaporized, leaving Abasi alone once again.

Proudman sat at his desk and watched the television in disbelief. Abasi had defeated the weaker Republican offering handily. It wasn't Abasi's victory that caused Proudman to shake his head, but the fact that America had fallen for the Abasi rhetoric so completely; while at the same time the Republican base decided not to turn out in support of their less than conservative candidate. In Proudman's estimation, the next four years would be hard. "It's all in Your hands now, Lord," Proudman said aloud.

Proudman's pocket vibrated, breaking his disbelieving gaze at the TV screen. He dug in his pocket for his iPhone and slid his finger over the screen to answer it. It was his good friend Simon Cross. "Doctor Cross, I presume!"

"Greetings, Reverend!"

"To what do I owe the honor of this call, Doctor?"

"Ha! Good to hear your voice, you old war dog!"

"Likewise, Doc. Have you overturned all the rocks in Israel yet?"

"Indeed! I was actually calling to offer my condolences about your elections. What in the devil is going on with you Yanks? Never thought I'd see a card-carrying Socialist in the White House."

"Neither did I, my friend. Dark days ahead I'm afraid."

"Indeed. Indeed." Simon Cross paused as he commiserated with Geoffrey Proudman for a few reflective moments. "So, mate... anything I can do to ease your pain?"

"Sure there is. Tell me you're headed stateside with your beautiful bride."

"As a matter of fact..."

"Yes! When?"

"Well, if you and Angelica can put us up for a few days, we'd like to fly in to Houston and spend Christmas... longer if you can stand us."

"We'd love it! Send me your flight schedule and we'll get you at Bush Intercontinental. Angelica will be thrilled."

"Excellent! Can hardly wait!"

"Same here, my friend! See you soon!"

"Indeed you will, Padre! Chin up! God is in control! Bye for now!"

"Yes, He is! And praise God for that! Bye, Doc." Proudman felt better. It had been far too long since he had seen his good friends Simon and Rachel. He picked up the television remote and turned off the giddy talking head as she typically and un-professionally gushed and gloated over the election results once again. "Got to tell Angelica the news," he thought. "She's gonna love it!" He texted her:

"Guess who's coming to visit?"

"Umm... no idea?"

"C'mon...guess!"

"Your mom?"

"Nope."

"Umm... Idk. Just tell me."

"Simon and Rachel!"

"Woo Hoo! When?"

"Next month. For Christmas."

"Yay! Sooo excited!"

"Me too. Ok gotta run. Love you."

"Love you too. Bye."

Geoffrey's spirits were lifted. He had been extraordinarily busy recently and hadn't realized just how much he had missed his friends. It would be good to have them in his home for a while, and over Christmas no less. He tried to focus his attention back on next week's sermon, but his mind drifted back to Israel and *The Gathering*. So many lives changed for Jesus, so many saved… and yet there was still so much darkness in the world. In fact, things worsened every day. And now, with the apparent shift in American values… the numbers of people who seemed lost and without hope were increasing rapidly. Many, Proudman feared, had placed their hope in Abasi instead of in Christ where it would make for some actual change. Obviously there was so much more work to be done. Proudman prayed that there was still time.

Proudman's thoughts continued to drift. He thought of his sons, C.P. and Alex, both about to embark on military careers. What would Abasi's election mean to their futures? Would a socialist regime in America be so at odds with the Constitution that it would force those in uniform, those who swore an oath to support and defend it against all enemies, foreign and domestic, to rise up against their own government? Was the thought so far-fetched? Proudman wondered what decisions his sons might be forced to make in the course of their careers.

Proudman's time in uniform seemed so much more straight-forward. Locate, close with and destroy the enemy... simple instructions. No fuss, no muss. Get in, wreak havoc on the enemy, then get out. Easy. Proudman's thoughts transported him back in time... *Visibility was zero. Sand blew everywhere. The sun was shining somewhere, just not where Proudman was. The burning oil wells had turned day into night and the wind-driven sand found its way into every crevice, every hole in Proudman's goggles, every gap in the scarf he had tied over his nose and mouth. He could feel the grit in his teeth and the distinct taste of petroleum coated his tongue. He wanted to spit, but that would mean lifting the scarf and compounding the problem.*

"Corporal Klark, let's have the team dismount and set up a perimeter. I don't want to run up on the enemy in these conditions."

"Aye, sir."

"And let's make sure to dig in deep. The knuckleheads are getting lazy and digging their holes too shallow. If we take arty or missiles out here in the open, they're gonna want to have lots of dirt above their heads."

"Aye, sir."

"And, Klark... I expect com between the holes. Don't skimp on running the landlines."

"Aye, sir."

"Well, what's keeping you, Klark? Go, go, go!"

"Aye, sir!"

Proudman watched Klark disappear into the darkness before grabbing his e-tool and dismounting the hummer. He pulled his compass off of his web gear and oriented himself toward the direction he believed the Iraqis to be. He pulled his k-bar from its sheath and drove it into the sand up to the hilt. He placed the compass next to it and drove his bayonet along the invisible azimuth about eighteen inches from the k-bar so that the compass needle pointed toward the bayonet. In this way, he could quickly orient himself from his fighting hole, once he had it dug.

When Corporal Klark returned to the hummer, he found Proudman putting the finishing touches on a roomy, two-man fighting hole. Klark jumped in and reported, "Perimeter is set, sir. Holes on point, rear and flanks. Deep holes, sir."

"Excellent. Tell me something, Klark... do you hear bells?"

"Bells, sir?"

"Like metal clanking sounds?"

Both Marines stopped and listened intently. It was hard to hear anything but the rushing wind and sand, but just above the din was a definite metallic clanking. Klark wired in the field phone and cranked it to get the signal to the other phones on the landline. "Anyone hear a clanking sound?"

"This is point. We hear it out in front of us. Sounds like it's getting closer."

"Sir, point says they hear it out front and getting closer."

"Tell them to look sharp and lock and load. There are no friendlies out here so whoever it is, they're not welcome in this perimeter!"

"Aye, sir. Point, if they try to come in, kill them."

Proudman and Klark hunkered down in their hole and waited with their gaze intently in the direction of the Marines on point. A shout of, "Halt! Who goes there!" pierced through the din and after a short pause, the sound of M-16s opening up in burst mode. Thirty seconds later the shots ceased and the clacker on the field phone sounded.

"Talk to me, point," Klark ordered.

"I think we killed them. Should we recon?"

"Sir, they got them. Should they go check?"

"Tell them to sit tight and stay alert. We'll recon when the wind stops."

"Point, sit tight and keep alert. Wait for orders."

"Roger that."

Time stopped. Proudman and Klark gazed into the darkness for what seemed like days. The uneasy feeling of the unknown crept into Proudman's consciousness. "Who had they killed? Were there more on the way? How long would they have to wait? Would the wind and sand ever stop?" As suddenly as it had started, the wind subsided and a small break appeared in the dense smoke clouds above. A ray of light shone through the smoke, as if God had pierced the darkness and emerged from the cloud with all His glory. Proudman rolled out of his fighting hole and made his way to the point position, where he saw his Marines staring, their gaze transfixed on the ray of light before them. The light shone down and illuminated a bloody heap of skin and fur about 15 meters beyond the Marines' position. A camel, with what resembled a cowbell around its neck, had wandered too close to the Marines' and had paid the ultimate price. Strangely to Proudman, he felt sorry for the camel. Even more strangely, he thought, is the fact that he knew he would not have felt at all sorry if they had killed actual human beings... provided they were Iraqis, of course. He sensed the other Marines were thinking along those lines as well.

Proudman shook his head in disbelief at the craziness of it all. "Let's mount up. Pass the word," he said quietly to the dumbfounded Marines in the hole below him.

Geoffrey drifted back into the present and shuddered with the usual chill that those recollections always provided. Thankfully, his sleep was more peaceful these days and the nightmares less frequent, but when the workload elevated his stress level, his memories tended to haunt him. And Proudman couldn't help but feel that the workload was about to rise exponentially with Abasi's victory. When times are tough, Proudman knew, the people become seekers. He was determined that New Covenant Church would be ready to meet them with open arms and the full-on gospel message. Real hope. Real change. For real people.

The preacher's eyes focused on the computer screen in front of him. He wanted to finish the sermon, but the words just wouldn't come. "God," he prayed. "I can't do this without you. None of it. Not this sermon, not this church, not this ministry, not this life you've given me." As he uttered the prayer, the thought came to him...

"Worship me, Geoffrey. Only through fellowship with Me will you have inspiration, strength, endurance."

Proudman recognized the still, small voice of his Lord. He knew that God spoke softly to him, not because God was small, but because He was close. Proximity was intimacy. Proudman reached for his Native American flute. The wood felt cool and smooth in his hands. He wetted his lips with his tongue to get a proper seal and exhaled gently into the instrument, producing a low, mellow tone. The notes came slowly and gently and drifted up like smoke from an altar, an offering of worshipful music to God.

As Proudman's music turned to prayer, Angelica softly opened the door. "Uh-oh," she said seeing Proudman with the flute in his hands. She knew the flute only came into play when the weight of the world was pressing down on her husband's shoulders. "What's on your mind, sailor?"

"Sailor? Do I look like I wear skirts to you, Ma'am?" Proudman said in his roughest jarhead tone.

"Now, I'd pay money to see that!" Angelica shot back. "Seriously, preacher man... what's troubling you?" Angelica sat on the couch across from the desk and curled her legs up underneath her.

"Just overwhelmed by the monumental task of saving the world," Geoffrey stretched as he answered.

"Well, maybe you could just concentrate on one soul at a time and while you're at it, remember, it's not your responsibility to save them. That's on God. All you have to do is share the message."

"True enough." Proudman rose from his desk and moved onto the couch next to Angelica. "You always know how to put my wheel back on course. Thank you, Babe."

"No worries. It's what I do. It's how I roll." Angelica leaned into him. He kissed her softly and she responded passionately. Angelica loved the chemistry God had created between them. Such fire. Such intensity. She reveled in it. She broke from their kiss, fanning herself as she did. "Mercy, preacher. We better take this show on the road before things get way out of hand."

Proudman chuckled. "Yeah. What if we got carried away and old Jim poked his head inside the office needing something!?"

"Ha! That would take him to Sunday school for sure! He'd get a real education!"

The pair dissolved in laughter at the thought of being interrupted by a vestry member like good old Jim. Such a perfect love they had for each other. Christ-centered. A holy marriage, which gave them freedom to live life and live it abundantly! The couple made their way out of the church, arm-in-arm; their laughter filling the empty building as they went.

chapter

FOUR

For many deceivers have gone out into the world, those who do not acknowledge Jesus Christ as coming in the flesh. This is the deceiver and the antichrist.

-2 John 1:7

Proudman jammed a K-cup into the coffee maker and pressed the button, setting the technological marvel into action. "One-touch go-juice," he said out loud. As he watched the hot, brown liquid dispense into the waiting mug, there was no question in Geoffrey's mind that this machine was the best $150 he'd ever spent. Black coffee was perhaps his biggest vice, and Proudman grasped the warm, ceramic mug of fresh brew with both hands, breathing in the aromatic steam, grateful to God for having created such a gratifying, pleasurable experience. He licked his lips before carefully setting them on the hot rim of the mug. He sipped the coffee slowly, taking in as much cool air as coffee to prevent a blistered tongue.

He made his way to the patio door where Coco and Daisy were waiting somewhat impatiently to go outside. Coco's tail thumped rhythmically on the hardwood floor in anxious anticipation of her morning freedom in the backyard. Proudman opened the door and followed the dogs out onto the patio. The air was brisk and the sun was just now casting a pink and orange glow on the last of the fall leaves still on the trees. A foursome of golfers putted on the third green at the edge of Proudman's yard, just beyond the pond where many a golf ball ended its short-lived career. This was Geoffrey's favorite time of the day. Each morning, he would take his coffee and sit on the patio and seek God's face. He could pray anytime, anywhere, but this time and place seemed uniquely set apart to him.

Proudman watched Coco run from tree to tree, eyes skyward, ever hopeful that one of the many squirrels taunting her would somehow misjudge an acrobatic leap between branches and end up on the ground where she could get hold of it in her massive pit bull jaws. "Crazy dog, you're just wishful thinking." Proudman chuckled at Coco's consistent determination despite years of never having managed to taste squirrel.

Moving his attention away from the dog's antics, Geoffrey took a last swallow of coffee, which had cooled all too quickly in the cold morning air, and turned his full focus on conversing with his God. "Abba, You are worthy of honor and glory and praise. So I lift up my eyes to You. Quiet my soul, Father, and lead me to the foot of the cross. There, I lay myself down, putting my will aside so that You can fill me up with Your Holy Spirit. Abba, pour out Your loving kindness to me. Extend Your grace and mercy to me this morning as You do every morning. Father, I belong to You. Create in me a clean heart and use me today as an instrument for advancing the kingdom of heaven. In Jesus' name I pray. Amen."

Geoffrey soaked in the quiet. Daisy lay at his feet, resting her paw on Proudman's foot. The golden retriever was all about human contact, and Proudman marveled at how just a touch was enough to keep her content and at peace. Coco, the more energetic pit bull, required more deliberate interaction and approval. How like people they were in that they had such distinct personalities, Proudman observed. As his thoughts wandered, the patio door opened and Angelica emerged with a cup of steaming coffee in one hand. The other hand brushed her hair from her face and then tugged the opening in her robe closed to keep out the chill.

"Brrrr," Angelica shivered at the temperature difference between the morning air and the warm bed she had just left.

"It feels spectacular," Geoffrey responded. "Come sit."

Angelica slid her feet into a pair of flip flops left at the patio door and slapped her way across the patio to Proudman's side. Geoffrey pulled a chair out for her and she nestled into it, removing her feet from the flip flops and placing them on Proudman's lap in one smooth motion. Geoffrey instinctively rubbed them with his warm hands, while Angelica sat back to enjoy her coffee, cradling it with both hands just under her nose.

"What time are Simon and Rachel due in?" Angelica managed between noisy sips of the hot, sweet, creamy liquid.

Geoffrey watched her sipping her coffee with great interest. Everything she did captivated him. "3:00 p.m. according to the itinerary Simon sent me."

"Yay!"

"Indeed." Geoffrey did his best Simon impersonation.

"Indeed." Angelica attempted Simon's signature word as the couple dissolved in laughter. "It will be good to have them here for a while."

Geoffrey sat back in his chair and continued watching Angelica as she sipped her coffee. He smiled at her and she flashed a cheesy grin over the rim of her coffee mug. Coco gave up her fascination with the taunting squirrels and sat next to Proudman, laying her head on his lap, ears cocked in anticipation of a quality head scratching. "What do you want, crazy, needy pup?" Geoffrey teased. He relented and began rubbing the dog's head. Coco let out an audible sigh and Angelica chuckled at the sound. "She turned out to be a good dog," Geoffrey said as he continued to scratch Coco's head.

"Yup. Proof that pit bulls have a bad rep," Angelica offered. "Hard to believe we've had her for, what is it now, four years? Ever since we came stateside from Israel..."

"She was a scrawny pup at the rescue shelter. Something about her eyes, I think, just said, 'I'm the one. Take me home.'" Geoffrey mused. Angelica sipped.

"Well look at who turned out to be a dog lover!" Angelica loved this aspect of Geoffrey's character. He cared about all living things, except maybe spiders... and roaches... and mosquitos... most bugs, generally.

"I appreciate loyalty and unconditional love," Geoffrey responded. "Dogs have that. Other than that, all they are good for is eating, sleeping and pooping."

Angelica rolled her eyes, then tilted her head up and closed them, allowing the sun to warm her face while her husband warmed her feet and her heart. "God is so good," she said quietly.

"All the time." Geoffrey followed Angelica's example and tilted his face up toward the sun.

❧

Doctors Simon and Rachel Cross made their way to the KLM baggage claim area at George Bush Intercontinental Airport – Houston. The flight from Tel Aviv to Houston via Amsterdam had been a breeze, especially with all the amenities attached to their *World Business Class* tickets, courtesy of the university. Simon was convinced that air travel was only civilized if one traveled business class or better, and then only on international flights. Domestic flights, in any class, in Simon's estimation, were only just slightly better than a jaunt in a cattle car. It wasn't that Simon Cross was a snob... far from it. And he certainly wasn't a soft individual, one incapable of enduring trying conditions. He was a field archaeologist, after all, and had spent many a month in the desert, in harsh conditions that would make seasoned soldiers wince. He just wasn't a man willing to put up with the airline industry's general mistreatment of the economy traveler. Rachel was happy just to be traveling away from sand. She loved archaeology, but she was tired of the digs and needed a respite.

The couple arrived at baggage claim in time to see the first bags slide onto the carousel. Fifteen minutes later, Simon had both of his bags and three of Rachel's four in hand.

"Here it comes, Love!" Rachel pointed as she alerted Simon, "The blue canvas one with the band around it."

Simon tugged at the over-sized suitcase, wrestling it off of the carousel. "What, in the name of heaven, do you have packed away in here, my love?"

"Clothes, mostly... and gifts for the Proudman family."

"Indeed."

Simon stacked the luggage on a cart and pushed it laboriously to the customs area, with Rachel providing encouragement along the way. "It's just ahead, Simon, Love... almost there."

"Indeed." Simon huffed.

The U.S. Customs agent motioned the pair into the chute. "Passports please. Do you have anything to declare?" Another agent moved their luggage onto the table and unzipped one of Rachel's medium-sized suitcases.

"Of course he had to pick the one with my undergarments," Rachel said under her breath into Simon's ear.

"Nothing this trip," Simon responded to the agent's question as he reached into his inside jacket pocket for their passports. "It'll be fine, Love." Simon said quietly back to Rachel.

"Come again?" The customs agent held his hand to his ear indicating he hadn't heard Simon clearly.

"Oh, no... I was just reassuring my wife that it's common procedure for your man to be sifting through her knickers... er... ah... I mean..."

"He's right, Ma'am. We sift through everybody's knickers. What is your business in the United States, Dr. Cross?"

"Indeed... Um, just visiting friends for the holidays."

"Very good, Mr. and Mrs. Cross. Enjoy your stay. Welcome to the United States."

"Indeed. And that's Doctors Cross, my good man."

"Very good, Doctors Cross. Welcome to the United States." The agent held out the passports to Simon and smiled.

Simon took the passports and touched them to his forehead in a sort of salute as he smiled back at the agent. He dragged the bags off the table and dropped them heavily onto the cart. "Off we go, Love. We're official now." Rachel smiled sheepishly at the agents as she followed Simon away from the security stand and out into the terminal.

"That was sort of embarrassing," Rachel complained to Simon. "I mean having my frillies rifled through by some strange man."

"I doubt he even noticed they were frillies, Love. They do that a few hundred times a day and if it doesn't look like contraband, they don't pay any attention to it."

"Maybe so, Simon, but I'm washing all my frillies when we get to Angelica and Geoffrey's."

"If it will make you feel less violated, my love. In fact, if it will make you feel better, we can go to a frilly store and get you all new knickers."

"Yes. Yes it would, Simon."

"Indeed."

❧

Angelica and Geoffrey pulled into the arriving flights lane in front of the international terminal just as Simon and Rachel emerged from the terminal's automatic doors. Geoffrey rolled down the car window and waved briskly, catching Rachel's attention.

"There they are, there they are!" Rachel said excitedly. "Come this way, Simon, they're right there!"

"Right behind you, Love." Simon was relieved that the baggage drudgery was almost over. "Next time I'm putting my foot down and drawing the line at one bag and a carry-on each," he thought to himself. The truth was that whatever Rachel desired, he would gladly give her.

Geoffrey wheeled the car up to the curb as close to Simon and Rachel as the line of waiting cars would allow. Angelica could hardly wait for Geoffrey to put the car in park so that she could jump out and run to Rachel and hug her neck. "Hi! I can't believe you're here!" Angelica squealed as she kissed Rachel's cheeks. "And, Simon! How are you? So good to see you!" Angelica latched on to Simon's neck as she had Rachel's.

Geoffrey embraced Rachel with a peck on the lips and a warm hug. "Welcome." He said into her ear. He then turned to Simon and the two exchanged bear hugs and claps on the back. "Good to see you, old man!"

"Bloody good to see you, mate!" Simon responded. "Bloody good, indeed!"

Rachel leaned into Angelica and quipped, "Such manly hugs!"

Angelica joined in, "Complete with the obligatory bro-slaps on the back!"

The women laughed together. Instantly they had re-bonded and become comfortable. It was as if they had never been apart.

"They're at it already, mate." Simon nudged Geoffrey.

"Didn't take long at all, did it?" Geoffrey responded with a grin. "Well, let's get you loaded up and head to the house!"

"Indeed!"

❦

APARTMENT OF PRESIDENT-ELECT ANWAR MUHAMMAD ABASI, JR. WASHINGTON, D.C.

Abasi was not used to sharing his apartment with Secret Service agents. He understood the need now that he was President-elect, but suddenly his privacy was limited and the agents were always underfoot. Instead of simply coming home and plopping into his recliner, now the detail had to check everything and everybody between the doorman and the apartment before he could even exit the limo. Then they had to check the apartment, physically and electronically. There was a 24-hour physical presence outside his door, and the entire building was patrolled from basement to roof whenever he was present. If that weren't enough, a smaller detail remained onsite even when he was not on the premises. Of course, all of this was temporary. After the inauguration, he would occupy the White House with his family. His wife, Rochelle, and their two daughters had remained in their Chicago home during his time as a senator, with only occasional trips to visit him. With all of the security and logistics, it was better, Abasi thought, that they were not in D.C. now.

"You're all secure, Sir." The Secret Service agent in charge of his detail almost clicked his heels together as he spoke.

"Thank you, er..."

"Agent Jameson, Sir."

"Thank you, Agent Jameson." Abasi hadn't learned their names yet. Quite frankly he viewed them as a nuisance, so he hadn't really made an effort. Abasi watched Agent Jameson as he closed the apartment door behind him. He sighed heavily as he slid into his recliner and reached for his iPhone. He slid his finger across the screen to unlock it and then instinctively touched the four-digit code sequence to reveal the app icons. He hit the phone button and touched Rochelle's name and waited as the phone connected.

"Hello, Anwar. 'Bout time you called home." Rochelle's tone was less than friendly. "You think just because you went and got yourself elected President that you don't have responsibilities back home. May I remind you that you have two daughters who, at this point, are wondering who their daddy is... and if you think..."

"Hold on, hold on now! I'm calling now, aren't I, Rochelle? You have no idea what my day has been like, and the last thing I need when I do finally get a minute to myself is an angry woman on the other end of the phone giving me grief! So, go simmer down a minute while I talk to my girls. Put one of them on the phone, if you please!" Abasi could hear the angry sigh as Rochelle called his daughters, Amelia and Sade', to the phone.

"Are you and Dad fighting again?" Anwar heard Amelia ask her mother.

"They always fight." He heard Sade' chime in.

"We're not fighting. We're discussing." Rochelle still could not get her angry tone under control.

"Sounds like fighting to me." Sade' retorted.

"Mind your business!" Rochelle scolded.

"When we moving in to the White House, Daddy?" Amelia was the first to pick up the phone.

"After New Year's."

"Why we gotta wait?"

"Because Daddy's got to be inaugurated before we can move in."

"Oh. Okay, hurry and get *innagrated* then, love you. Bye!"

"Wait... hmm. Gone."

"Hey, Mister Prez!" Sade' sang into the phone.

"Hey, Sade'. How's my girl?"

"Good, Dad. You coming home for the holidays?"

"You betcha."

"Good. Bring me something from Washington, please."

"Will do, Hun. Love you."

"Love you too, Dad." Sade' pushed the "END" button on her mom's phone causing Abasi's phone to disconnect as well.

"Oh well. Didn't really want to talk to the angry "B" anyway," Anwar said aloud. He reached for the television remote, hoping Rochelle would not hit the callback button. She did not.

HOME OF ROCHELLE AND ANWAR ABASI, JR. CHICAGO.

"Sade', you hung up on your Father before I had a chance to speak to him."

"I know. You'd just yell at him anyway."

"You, young lady, are too big for your britches. Now get upstairs and get ready for bed. Now!" Rochelle watched as her daughter huffed her way up the stairs. "And brush your teeth!"

"Whatever."

"And do NOT 'whatever' me; and do NOT speak to me in that disrespectful tone!"

Rochelle moved into the kitchen and put the water on for tea. Maybe some chamomile would calm her down before calling Anwar back. The stress of being a mom and a senator's wife was sometimes too much for her, not because she wasn't

capable of either role, but rather because she didn't particularly like being either one. For one thing, she knew she could be
a better senator than Anwar. For another, she knew she could
have been a person of tremendous influence if she hadn't had
children. Her life and her youth were passing her by, and that
made her angry. But, she had to admit that this new role as
First Lady might have the advantages she was so desperate
for... prestige, power... it was all about to be hers.

The tea kettle began to whistle and the shrillness slowly
overtook Rochelle's thoughts until she snapped back to reality.
She pushed back from the kitchen table and attempted to rise
from her chair. Panic invaded her as she suddenly felt pressed
into the wooden seat. Again she attempted to push herself up,
but the downward force on her body increased. A scream formed
in her core, but the downward force prevented it from escaping.
Her breathing was labored and she felt she might pass out. As she
sat helpless, Abaddon materialized in the chair across the square
wooden table from her. Rochelle's eyes widened in horror as the
pasty-white figure became flesh.

"I will release you if you promise to remain calm so as not
to alert the children upstairs," Abaddon said softly. "And let me
just assure you that you most definitely don't want them to in-
terrupt us. Can you sit there calmly if I let you go?"

Rochelle nodded rapidly.

"No, I need you to say the words so that I know you comprehend."

"Yes, I can sit calmly," Rochelle shivered the sentence into the air, which she realized was much colder now.

"Good." Abaddon waved his fingers slightly and the pressure on Rochelle subsided. She took in a much needed breath of chilled air.

"Who... who are you?"

"I am many things, child. But most essentially for this conversation, you should know that I am your husband's father. You should also know that I am capable of lifting him, and you, to great heights... or I can crush you both and send you to oblivion for all eternity. Do I have your full attention?"

"You do." Rochelle's thoughts began to formulate how she could use this unexpected turn of events to her advantage.

"Excellent." Abaddon easily read her thoughts and smiled. "You will be most useful I think. Listen carefully. Your husband, my son the politician, is where he is now by my orchestration. We both know that he is an incompetent boob when left to his own devices. So, now that he is about to be the most powerful human being on the planet, I cannot allow him to function without a spine. And, since he does not possess one, you will be that spine. Understand?"

Rochelle nodded.

"Again with the head bobbing. Let me hear the words, child!"

"I understand."

"Splendid. One more thing. I'm going to give you some help. It's not that I doubt your abilities; you seem to be a perfectly angry dominant bitch in your own right, but you are human after all, and therefore, not trustworthy." Abaddon closed his eyes and spoke a name into the darkness of the Abyss, "Izebel."

The icy room became colder still as a mist arose out of thin air. "Izebel," Abaddon chanted again. Gradually, the mist became more substantive and a female form appeared in the fog.

"Master," the translucent woman breathed out audibly.

"Jezebel. Welcome to Chicago," Abaddon mused, pleased with himself.

"Who is she?" Rochelle found her voice again.

"Someone familiar with getting her man to do exactly what I want them to do. Don't be rude, Jezebel... introduce yourself to our hostess."

"I am Jezebel, daughter of Ethbaal, King of the Siddonians, wife of Ahab, King of Israel."

"Rochelle, Jezzie here has a knack for killing prophets of God and manipulating her husband to do my bidding. A real talent, which, as it happens, I can use right now. So if you'd be so kind as to allow her to occupy your body along with you; that would be most excellent. So... go on then, scooch over a smidge and let Jezzie in there..."

Jezebel was on Rochelle in an instant. Rochelle squeaked unnaturally as Jezebel penetrated Rochelle's chest and climbed inside. Rochelle's body shook as her eyes rolled back into her head. She could feel Jezebel's presence in her mind, but it was more than just an invasion of her thoughts, it was an all-out takeover of her identity. Clearly, in her own body, Rochelle was no longer the dominant one. After a minute or two of violent spasms and abnormal contortions, Jezebel, the helpless Rochelle captive with her, rose and walked toward Abaddon.

"Well, Rochelle... Jezebel... or should we just call you Rochebel? Hmm? I want you to get a grip on my son and keep him from making a fool of himself. There is much to be done and I don't want his lack of intestinal fortitude slowing me down. Clear?"

"Clear, Master." Rochelle heard herself speak but knew she hadn't formed the words of her own will. "Relax, Rochelle. You will become accustomed to me. We shall be fast friends," Jezebel reassured Rochelle. "Now let's have that tea, yes?"

chapter

FIVE

Jesus wept.

-John 11:35

PROUDMAN HOME. CHRISTMAS EVE.

"What should I wear tonight, Angie?" I don't want to appear too casual, but then we will have a whole new television audience, so I don't want to appear too stuffy and unapproachable, do I?"

Angelica chuckled inwardly at her husband's questions. "I should be the one with the 'What do I wear tonight?' questions, shouldn't I? I mean, that's usually my line whenever we have a function to go to."

Riding the financial wave of the recent Bible-based television and theater epics, New Covenant Church had been invited by the FOX Broadcasting Company to broadcast their Christmas Eve service live, nationally, and the Proudman household was in full-motion as they got ready to depart for the church. Likewise, the Cross family was gearing up for the television event, as Simon and Rachel set out their clothes on the queen-sized bed in the guest bedroom.

"This is so exciting," Rachel spoke to Simon's reflection in her dressing table mirror.

"Indeed." Simon replied as he fumbled with the buttons on his dress shirt. "How do you suppose Geoffrey managed prime airtime on a major network for a Christmas Eve service?"

"Good question. It must have been expensive for whoever invited them, don't you think?"

"No doubt, but I suppose the network thinks the sponsorship opportunities are worth the expense. You recall the masses that tuned-in to '*The Bible*' series a few months ago, right?" Rachel nodded into the mirror as she flat-ironed her lengthy hair. "Well perhaps that success has something to do with this endeavor."

"Well, let's just pray that Geoffrey's message will reach thousands for Christ tonight!"

"Indeed! That would be most wonderful!"

Geoffrey opted for a pair of khaki trousers, a wine-colored, button-down shirt and a medium brown sport coat. He placed a neatly-folded, burgundy handkerchief in the breast pocket of his jacket and retrieved his father's Rolex from the dresser. He didn't wear the watch every day as it was just too much jewelry for a preacher, Proudman thought. But tonight was a special occasion and he wanted a reminder of his dad with him. It had been many years since he had gone home to be with Jesus, but Proudman still missed him daily. Geoffrey glanced at himself in the mirror and then moved behind Angelica at her vanity table where she was applying eye makeup with the aid of a lighted vanity mirror. He bent at the waist and kissed the top of Angelica's head. Her dark hair had a light, clean fragrance, which he inhaled deeply. He kissed her again. "I'm going to look over my sermon in the study until it's time to go."

"Ok, love. I wish Alex were here to hear it." Angelica voiced what Geoffrey had been thinking. Their adopted son, Alex, had deployed not three weeks ago to Afghanistan with his Marine Reserve unit and they had yet to hear any word from him about his safe arrival and well-being.

"I wish that too. We need to keep him lifted up in prayer tonight. I know first-hand what Christmas in a combat zone is like. It can be considerably less than festive."

Proudman squeezed Angelica's shoulder reassuringly and left their master suite for his study. He sat in his leather office chair and opened his laptop, pressing the power button as he did so. As he waited for the computer to boot-up, he looked around his office and let his mind wander down rabbit trails created by the memorabilia adorning the walls. There were class photos from Artillery School at Fort Sill, and from his graduating class at the Episcopal Theological Seminary of the Southwest. There were framed photos of him next to a 155mm howitzer in the Iraqi desert, and next to the cross in the quadrangle outside the chapel window at the seminary. High on the wall, opposite his desk, above the windows, hung a display box with his Mameluke sword, the sword he wore as a Marine officer; its white ivory handle, gold hilt and long, curved blade shimmered in the light coming from his desk lamp. And above his desk, in a smaller display box, was his first pastor's stole, neatly folded to display the embroidered crosses at the ends. It was a gift from his mother, Beth, at his ordination, and he wore it faithfully for his first year of service. Twilight was falling, and the hues of pink and orange were streaming in through the floor-to-ceiling windows, bathing his entire office in a supernatural glow. The soft light had a calming effect, and Proudman closed his eyes and sat still, allowing God the space to speak to him if He would.

After a time, Geoffrey heard the still quiet voice of God break the silence in the room. There was no denying the power in the voice, whispered into his consciousness so as not to overwhelm him as it said, *"I will wipe away every tear from your eyes; and there will no longer be any death; there will no longer be any mourning, or crying, or pain; the first things have passed away. Behold, I am making all things new."* Proudman meditated on the words when a harsh light flashed across his eyelids, jarring him into the world again. He realized the rudely interrupting light was the low beams of an automobile pulling into his driveway. Geoffrey rose from his desk and walked to the window and peered through the open blinds. He did not recognize the car, but it had the official look of a government sedan. His heart froze as he saw two officers, decked out in Marine dress blues emerge from the vehicle. They retrieved their covers from the back seat and placed them crisply on their heads. Proudman rushed from his office to the front door and opened it before the Marines reached the front porch.

"Reverend Proudman?"

"Yes," Proudman answered while searching their faces to see if his fears were confirmed.

"May we come inside, Sir?"

"Of course. Please." Proudman opened the door wide and allowed the two officers, a Captain and a First Lieutenant, to enter. "Please, have a seat. Before you say anything, I know why you're here. Let me gather my family so that we can all hear it together."

"Of course, Reverend," the Captain said softly.

Proudman walked quickly back to the master bedroom and touched Angelica's face gently with the backs of his fingers. "I need you to come with me," he said to her gently. Angelica sensed that something was not right in the tone of his voice, but she didn't question him and let him lead her by the hand out of the room.

As they passed the guest bedroom, Geoffrey stopped and knocked gently. Simon opened the door with a jovial, "We're just about ready, mate. Rachel's just trying on her third dress..." Simon's voice trailed off and he could tell that Geoffrey's eyes were tearing up. "What's up, mate?"

"Get Rachel and join us in the living room." Simon turned and retrieved Rachel from the walk-in closet and they followed Geoffrey and Angelica down the hall and into the living room. Geoffrey sat Angelica down in his favorite chair across from the couch where the two Marines sat stiffly in their blues. Angelica's heart sank as she took in the scene. Rachel moved to her side and sat next to her in the over-sized chair.

Geoffrey held up his finger, telling the Marines to hold on for a moment longer as he went into the game room to get Missy, Freddie and C.P., who were busily blasting each other and every-thing that moved, playing *Call of Duty* on the widescreen as they waited to go to the church. "Missy, Freddie, C.P., put the game down and come with me." The brothers and sister would typically have responded to such a request with any number of objections, but the quivering of Geoffrey's voice told them that they need-ed to obey this time without hesitation. As Missy and her older brothers settled onto the big brown ottoman in the center of the living room, Proudman nodded to the Marine Captain, indicat-ing that everyone was present and able to receive his message.

The Captain began, "Reverend and Mrs. Proudman, We regret to inform you that your son, Corporal Alex Morgan-Proudman, was killed in action by an improvised explosive device in the Helmand Province in Afghanistan. While I don't have extensive details of the events that took place, the local Chaplain will follow up with you in the next few days. Our deepest sympathies for your loss." The two Marines rose slowly and excused themselves, leaving the speechless family in a surreal state of drift.

"What just happened?" Missy spoke first. "Did he just say that Alex is dead? Tell them to come back in here and take that back! Dad, tell them to come back here and take that back! My brother is not dead! My brother just left here two and a half weeks ago and he is gonna FaceTime me as soon as he gets settled in over there! Tell them to get back in here and take it back!" Angelica could barely see through her tears to get to Missy's side, but she did so anyway. Missy clung to her and buried her face into Angelica's shoulder as reality forced its way into her consciousness. Sobs took control of her. Rachel joined them by wrapping them both in her arms. C.P. preferred to deal with the news in solitude, but his emotions smothered him as he slammed the door to his room and collapsed on his bed, pulling the blankets over his head to shut out the world. Freddie headed for the back patio with Daisy and Coco, choosing to process the bad news in the fresh air in the company of his four-legged companions. Simon embraced a shell-shocked Geoffrey, and the group sat in silent and suspended agony, wondering if the peace that passes all understanding would ever kick in.

"Hey, mate. Would you like me to make some calls and cancel the televised Christmas Eve service?" Simon broke the hour-long silence. "We should let the network know something, as air time is only 90 minutes away."

Geoffrey's glazed expression slowly acknowledged Simon's question and he moved his lips, but no words came out. He tried again, managing to find his voice. "No. I think now, more than ever, we need to press on and proclaim the gospel. Otherwise, Satan wins tonight. I won't allow that. I owe Alex that much." Geoffrey looked at Angelica, Missy and Rachel, tightly bundled on the over-sized chair. "Rachel, will you stay with them while I go to the church?"

"Of course."

"No. I'm going too," Angelica managed through a raspy voice. "I'm going. Period." She said more firmly, making sure no one would even think about trying to object. Geoffrey nodded.

"I'm going too," Missy said just as firmly. Geoffrey started to object anyway, but Missy cut him off immediately. "I said, I'm going, Dad." Geoffrey nodded.

"I'll pull the car around," Simon offered.

"No need, my friend. FOX is sending a car. Should be here anytime now," Geoffrey glanced at his father's watch. His heart skipped a beat as he did so, as if the scab of that old wound were somehow freshly opened by this new pain of Alex's tragic, untimely demise.

Missy disengaged from her mom's embrace and went back to check on her brothers. "C.P., we're going to the church," Missy said through his bedroom door. "Are you coming, or do you just want to stay here? C.P.?"

"I'm staying," C.P. replied through the blankets.

"Okay. I'll check on you when we get back, okay?" Missy listened for a moment, but there was no reply. She started to repeat herself, but then decided it best to leave him alone. She knew from experience that her brother dealt with pain internally. There was no point in trying to get him to interact with anyone. He would reach out only when he was ready. Missy grabbed her coat and made her way to the patio where Freddie sat rubbing Daisy's head while Coco paced around the wrought iron fence. "We're going to church, Freddie. Are you coming or staying?"

"I'm staying with the dogs," Freddie said quietly.

"Okay. I'll come find you when we get back." Freddie nodded and Missy turned and left the patio where she met the others at the limo in the driveway. "C.P. and Freddie are staying here." Angelica nodded.

The short drive to the church was one of deafening silence. Proudman wondered how he would ever get through the message with his heart cut open and bleeding. He looked around the expansive interior of the stretched-out Hummer. Every face was tear-soaked. Angelica's newly applied mascara was streaking down her face. Simon and Rachel, strong beforehand, now wept openly for their dearest friends' pain. Geoffrey's mind searched the scriptures, and the only verses that came to mind were from John's gospel: *"When Jesus therefore saw her weeping, and the Jews who came with her also weeping, He was deeply moved in spirit and was troubled, and said, "Where have you laid him?" They said to Him, "Lord, come and see." Jesus wept. So the Jews were saying, "See how He loved him!" But some of them said, "Could not this man, who opened the eyes of the blind man, have kept this man also from dying?"* Geoffrey put his face in his hands and wept.

The limousine pulled in front of the church and the driver held the rear door as the Proudman and Cross families disembarked. Simon paused to tip the driver before following behind the group into the church. Rachel, Angelica and Missy hurried to Geoffrey's office to avoid having to interact with friends and church members. It would be awkward to have to pretend all was well, when it was far from well.

Geoffrey proceeded to the sanctuary where the praise band was running through their set before service time. He looked at his father's watch and felt the anguish attempt to surface once again. "Lord, give me strength," he said under his breath. Geoffrey motioned to Matthew, the worship leader, who cut the band off and walked to the edge of the platform, crouching to hear what Proudman wanted. "I know you have a set worked up already with a Christmas theme, but I wonder if you could indulge me with a change for the offering and the invitational."

"No problem. What's the change?"

"Could you do Jon Foreman's *'House of God Forever'* for the offering and then Jeremy Camp's *'There Will Be a Day'* for the invitational?"

"Sure thing. Those are kind of heavy. Everything okay?"

"No, my friend. Everything is most assuredly not okay. But we'll get through it."

Matthew nodded and decided not to press. He turned back to the worship team and announced the change. A few minutes later the soulful sounds of *'House of God Forever'* reverberated off of the sanctuary walls. Proudman knelt at a prayer riser and prayed for strength to get him through the broadcast. "Lord, just get me to the other side of this service. Abba, Father, hold me up lest I fall on my face during this message. I can't do this without you." As Proudman prayed, the last chorus of Foreman's song echoed in his head and in his heart:

God is my shepherd

I won't be wanting

I won't be wanting

He makes me rest

In fields of green

Like quiet streams

Even while I'm walking

Through the valley

Of death and dying

I will not fear

'Cause you are with me

You're always with me

The song comforted Geoffrey and he could sense a glimmer of that illusive peace promised in God's Word. The people were starting to come into the sanctuary now, and Proudman slowly got off his knees, making his way behind the platform to wait for the worship music to start the FOX broadcast. He didn't want to see anybody beforehand. He knew if he did, he would lose his focus and not be able to get through the service. This broadcast was too important now to fail. It had become bigger than just an outreach mission. This was a major battle in the war on Satan. He sensed the power of the Holy Spirit well-ing up in him. This message would be for Alex and for victory in Jesus Christ.

ABASI RESIDENCE. CHICAGO.

Anwar Abasi surfed through the cable channels looking for something to watch. Rochelle busied herself with chewing out the new nanny she had hired to take over the mundane task of dealing with the Abasi children. It wasn't that the nanny had done something incorrectly; it was just that Rochelle and her indwelt partner, Jezebel, were happiest when making others feel the weight of their wrath. Oddly enough, Anwar hadn't really noticed a change in Rochelle. She wore her Jezebel seamlessly.

Anwar paused on the local FOX affiliate and settled on watching the Christmas Eve special broadcast from New Covenant Church in Houston. Abasi liked to watch the Christian pastors. He got great pleasure in ridiculing them and poking fun at their typically animated speaking styles and their beliefs. He admittedly envied some of them for their oratory flair and ability to go on for 20 minutes or more without a teleprompter. "This should be amusing," he said to himself.

Abaddon materialized on the sofa adjacent to the chair where Anwar was just getting comfortable. Anwar shot up from his seat, startled once again by Abaddon's sudden entry. "Dammit, Father! Why must you do that?!"

"It's truly one of the perks of my existence; to pop in unannounced and scare the hell out of people."

Abasi settled back on to the chair and reached for his cocktail, draining the glass hoping to medicate his frazzled nerves. "So to what do I owe the pleasure of your company, Father?"

"Misery loves company. I thought I would share my misery with you on this most tragic of nights. I see you are not honoring your Islamic rules forbidding alcohol... a tad hypocritical, but then, I'm into that. Why don't you pour your old man one?"

"Ah, yes. Christmas Eve. Just another night to me," Anwar said matter-of-factly as he rose and went to the wet bar.

"Perhaps. But make no mistake, my son. This night changed everything. My life has been a living hell ever since."

"That's quite funny," Anwar handed Abaddon his drink before reclaiming his comfortable place in the chair. "So I understand why you hate Christians and Jews, but I don't understand why you are so tolerant of Muslims. I mean, it's not like they worship you. In fact, they think they are actually worshipping God."

"Precisely, my boy! They think they are worshipping God, when they are actually worshipping a fabrication of my imagination! They are worshipping an ancient pagan moongod whose image is fashioned after... wait for it...me! Ha ha! Islam is probably one of the most successful, if not the most successful, deceptions I have ever perpetrated against man-kind. Millions upon millions of souls; all delightfully lost and headed for the Abyss in a state of euphoric jihadist ignorance! Magnificent! And what's more, their evil little hearts will gleefully destroy Jews and Christians by the truckload all day long. Mark my words, son; they will be most useful and effi-cient killers when you finally get inside that big white house in Washington! Whatever you do, keep up the Islamic façade as long as possible."

"I intend to, I assure you."

"Excellent. Now what in blazes are you watching? A tel-evangelist?"

"Oh, in a manner of speaking, I suppose. It really is quite entertaining. They rant on and on about Jesus and salvation and other such nonsense, and I ridicule them and blow off steam. Great fun, really. Watch... you'll see."

"I suppose it would help ease my melancholy to ridicule a few Christian fools."

"That's the spirit." Abasi sipped his drink and turned up the volume a bit. "Cigar?" He reached for his humidor and flipped the lid open in front of Abaddon's pasty white face.

"Now you're talking. We might just make a man out of you yet." Abaddon selected a Cuban and reached into thin air, producing a trimmer. He trimmed the end of the cigar and sniffed the cigar along its entire length with a thin-lipped smile.

"Light?" Abasi flicked a table lighter, causing the torch to ignite in a 6-inch flame.

"Got my own," Abaddon replied as he ignited the cigar's end with the touch of his finger. The worship music started as the pair puffed away on their stogies. "Insipid drivel," Abaddon mouthed past his cigar at the music.

As soon as the worship set ended, Proudman mounted the platform. He smiled weakly at Angelica, having bravely taken her seat on the front row. Next to her sat a watery-eyed Missy, and on the other side of her sat an equally tearful Rachel. Each held one of Angelica's hands. Next to Rachel, Simon sat with an arm around Rachel and his eyes on Geoffrey, ready to be there should his friend need support of any kind.

Simon could only imagine that Geoffrey's pain was something akin to the pain he felt when he lost his first wife, Sarah, and their newborn child, so many years ago. It took many years and the love of the beautiful Rachel Rosenkranz to get past the pain.

The Reverend Proudman moved to the podium and scanned his notes. The FOX cameras added a new dimension to the otherwise familiar sanctuary, but his attention was only momentarily distracted by them. He adjusted the microphone on his earpiece and stepped into the center of the platform. "Pray with me," he said as he bowed his head and raised his arms.

"Abba, Father, use the meditations of my heart to voice the message You would have us know today. May this word honor You and glorify You as we pause to recognize the gift of Emmanuel, God with us, on this, the Eve of His birth. In His name we pray. Amen."

"Meditations of my heart. Such goo. I'll rip your bloody heart right out and have it with lentils, preacher man!" Abaddon scoffed at the television.

Geoffrey looked out at his congregation, easily a thousand strong on this special night, and felt a sense of responsibility blanket him. From his viewpoint, it seemed as if he could have a one-on-one conversation with every man, woman and child present. He could see their faces more clearly than he had ever seen them before in all his time on the platform. He began his sermon.

"We all know the significance of this night. The Bible says, in the gospel according to Luke:

'And it came to pass in those days, that there went out a decree from Caesar Augustus that all the world should be taxed.

² (And this taxing was first made when Cyrenius was governor of Syria.)

³ And all went to be taxed, every one into his own city.

⁴ And Joseph also went up from Galilee, out of the city of Nazareth, into Judaea, unto the city of David, which is called Bethlehem; (because he was of the house and lineage of David:)

⁵ To be taxed with Mary his espoused wife, being great with child.

⁶ And so it was, that, while they were there, the days were accomplished that she should be delivered.

⁷ And she brought forth her firstborn son, and wrapped him in swaddling clothes, and laid him in a manger; because there was no room for them in the inn.

⁸ And there were in the same country shepherds abiding in the field, keeping watch over their flock by night.

⁹ And, lo, the angel of the Lord came upon them, and the glory of the Lord shone round about them: and they were sore afraid.

¹⁰ And the angel said unto them, Fear not: for, behold, I bring you good tidings of great joy, which shall be to all people.

¹¹ For unto you is born this day in the city of David a Saviour, which is Christ the Lord.

¹² And this shall be a sign unto you; Ye shall find the babe wrapped in swaddling clothes, lying in a manger.

¹³ And suddenly there was with the angel a multitude of the heavenly host praising God, and saying,

¹⁴ Glory to God in the highest, and on earth peace, good will toward men.'

The Christmas Story, the celebration of the incarnation of God come to mankind in the form of a lowly baby. Fully God, yet fully human. You've heard me say many times from this pulpit that our salvation did not begin in the manger, but rather it has its origin before the very foundations of the world. So while we celebrate the human birth, immaculately conceived, of Jesus, I want you to remember that this night and the rest of the story of Jesus' life in the world were all conceived, just as immaculately, in the mind of an eternal God long before the first advent of our Savior.

Birthdays are traditionally marked with the giving of gifts. So I invite you to give a gift to our Lord Jesus tonight. 'What gift could I possibly give tonight, preacher? I mean I'm all tithed up and I'm going to put my special Christmas offering in the collection plate right after the offering song when you're done preaching! What could I possibly give over and above all that?' Well, I'll tell you, beloved. You can give the gift of obedience to your Savior. You can go out from here and spread the good news. You can honor Christ by honoring the Great Commission given to us in the Book of Matthew, where Jesus commands us to go and make disciples of all the nations!

'I'm not sure I can do that, preacher. I'm not good with words and public speaking and stuff.' Well, my response to that is to lovingly tell you to stop making excuses. Listen to me, now. I'm going to give you some tools so that everyone in this sanctuary and everyone watching on television will have the ability to go spread the good news of Christ's birth, life, death, and resurrection. Armed with these tools, you will be fully equipped to give Jesus the birthday gift He deserves because He is worthy. Are you ready? Get your Bibles and notepads handy; and hang on tight because I'm going to try and fit all of this in within our allotted television time slot!"

"This should be rich," Abasi quipped."

"That preacher... there is something familiar about him," Abaddon leaned forward trying to place from where he knew Proudman's face.

Geoffrey walked back to the podium and scanned his notes once again. He took a long pull of water from the glass on the podium and slowly made his way back to the center of the platform. The cameras followed his every step.

"What do you suppose is the single most formidable obstacle that Christ-followers encounter when attempting to share the gospel with others? If you've ever attempted to share your faith with anyone, then you already know the answer to that question: Fear.

Fear is a faith killer. What was it that kept the Israelites from crossing the river into the promised land? Fear. What was it that caused a nation of people to wander the desert for 40 years? Fear. What was it that caused an entire generation to die as nomads instead of crossing over into the land of milk and honey? Fear. The same fear that keeps the believer from sharing their faith! Fear of rejection. Fear of our own inadequacy and lack of understanding. Fear of ridicule. Fear of being odd or different. Fear kills faith. And Satan uses our fears and anxieties to quell the spread of the good news in the world. He does not have the power to alter or change or destroy the Word. He cannot touch the gospel message because he cannot dispel the Truth. But, he can and will use our human weakness, our fear, against us to prevent us from stepping out to boldly proclaim the gospel.

What conquers fear? Fear bows to only one thing... Divine Love. The love of God will drive out fear under any and all circumstances. As created people, we derive our strength from the receiving and giving of Love. The Bible says in 1 John 4:17-19 that, *'Whoever confesses that Jesus is the Son of God, God abides in him, and he in God. We have come to know and have believed the love which God has for us. God is love, and the one who abides in love abides in God, and God abides in him. By this, love is perfected with us, so that we may have confidence in the day of judgment; because as He is, so also are we in this world. There is no fear in love; but perfect love casts out fear, because fear involves punishment, and the one who fears is not perfected in love. We love, because He first loved us.'*

So you see, beloved, love casts out fear. In ancient times, just as they do today, the Jewish people would study the *Pentateuch*, the Five Books of Moses, which are the first books of the Torah. As Christians we know these books as the first five books of the Old Testament; Genesis, Exodus, Leviticus, Numbers, and Deuteronomy. Contained in Deuteronomy is the central prayer of the Jewish prayer book (the Siddur), known as The Shema': '*Shema' Yisrael, Adonai eloheinu (elo hey nu), Adonai echad.*'

'*Hear, O Israel! The Lord is our God, the Lord is one! You shall love the Lord your God with all your heart and with all your soul and with all your might. These words, which I am commanding you today, shall be on your heart. You shall teach them diligently to your sons and shall talk of them when you sit in your house and when you walk by the way and when you lie down and when you rise up. You shall bind them as a sign on your hand and they shall be as frontals on your forehead. You shall write them on the doorposts of your house and on your gates.*' (Deuteronomy 6:4-9)

So important is the love of God in the lives of the believer, that we are commanded to keep the commandment to love God on our hearts, teach it to our children and talk about it daily in our homes, in the morning when we wake up and in the evening before bed, so that it endures generation to generation. We should wear reminders of the commandment on our hands, so that we can see, and on our foreheads, so that others can see, and we should write them on the doorways and gates of our homes. Have you ever visited a Jewish home? Faithful Jews will have a mezuzot mounted to the door frames of their houses and inside each mezuzot is a scroll written in Hebrew containing The Shema'.

Why do I share this with you? Why is this important as we set out to share the love of Jesus Christ with our community?

As you go, you will inevitably encounter Satan's favorite obstacle. You will meet someone who needs to hear the good news. God will place that on your heart. And the devil will throw your natural fears and anxieties in front of you to discourage you from sharing the gospel. When that happens, I want you to remember who it is that sent you. I want you to remember the love He has for you, and the love you have for Him. And then I want you to know who it is you are ministering to...

If you walk anywhere outside the walls of New Covenant Church, you are likely to minister to everyday people. But, just who, exactly, are everyday people? They are whole families... or single moms. They are the working poor, or the recently laid off executive. They might have a mortgage or they might call the streets home. They might mow the lawn of the house next door to you, or they might own it and be struggling to keep it out of foreclosure. They are the person in the checkout line next to you at the grocery store, or the butcher who slices your meat. They might hand you your child's happy meal at the drive-through window or pour you more iced tea at your favorite restaurant.

The day care worker you trust with your toddler every day might be an everyday person, and many of your child's friends at school as well. They are your family members, your neighbors, your co-workers and fellow parishioners. Everyday people, thousands of them, are woven into the fabric of your community and you just never know who they might be and where you might encounter them as you go through your day. The fact is, at any given moment, any one of us might be in the same circumstances as everyday people. And, even more than that, for some everyday people, we might be their only point of access to the hope of Christ.

With all of that in mind, I want you to see the everyday people that you are sharing the gospel with as loveable... worthy of love, and worthy of compassion; made worthy not because of who they are, but because of <u>whose</u> they are. They are just like you and me. If that knowledge doesn't dispel the fear, then think of this Word from 2 Timothy 1:7: *'For God has not given us a spirit of timidity, but of power and love and discipline.'* We worship a mighty God, a God of power and strength and love and discipline, and He passes those qualities on to us in abundance. *'I can do all things through Him who strengthens me.'* (Philippians 4:13). If we can approach a God like that, surely we can find the courage through Christ to approach someone who is just like us! **If you can kneel before God, you can stand in front of anybody!**

So, I encourage you today to go with confidence and share the good news as we have been commanded to do by Christ Himself. Jesus said, *'All authority has been given to Me in heaven and on earth. Go therefore and make disciples of all the nations, baptizing them in the name of the Father and the Son and the Holy Spirit, teaching them to observe all that I commanded you; and lo, I am with you always, even to the end of the age.'* (Matthew 28:18-20)

There is no force on earth, no force in heaven that can keep God from advancing His kingdom, and by extension, nothing can keep you from accomplishing the kingdom work you have been called to do. We have the love of God on our side! *'If God is for us, who is against us? He who did not spare His own Son, but delivered Him over for us all, how will He not also with Him freely give us all things? Who will bring a charge against God's elect? God is the one who justifies; who is the one who condemns? Christ Jesus is He who died, yes, rather who was raised, who is at the right hand of God, who also intercedes for us. Who will separate us from the love of Christ? Will tribulation, or distress, or persecution, or famine, or nakedness, or peril, or sword? Just as it is written,*

"For Your sake we are being put to death all day long;

We were considered as sheep to be slaughtered."

But in all these things we overwhelmingly conquer [we are more than conquerors] through Him who loved us. For I am convinced that neither death, nor life, nor angels, nor principalities, nor things present, nor things to come, nor powers, nor height, nor depth, nor any other created thing, will be able to separate us from the love of God, which is in Christ Jesus our Lord.' (Romans 8:31-39)

If you will do this, Church... If you will go into the world and share this good news with all of the everyday people out there... Well, you will have dealt Satan such a mighty blow that he will retreat back to the pit of Hell with his tail between his legs and a cross branded into his pasty-white forehead! And to that I say, Go, therefore, in courage and love! Merry Christmas everyone!"

The praise band came in at full volume with a rocking version of *"Joy to the World"* as the credits rolled on the live broadcast.

Abaddon sat sneering at the television screen; his trembling hand covering the cross-shaped scar on his forehead, as the realization flooded over him. It was him. The holy man from *The Gathering*. He had a beard and his hair was more salt and peppered, but there was no mistaking his voice and the authority with which he preached. "It's him!" Abaddon seethed. "His message is deadly to our cause, Anwar. We must crush him and his church." Abaddon could barely see through his rage. "We must destroy all such churches and all those who preach the wretched gospel! When you take power, we must move swiftly to make all Christ-followers enemies of the state. I will not rest until every last one of them is rotting in the grave. If they want so badly to see their Savior, we shall arrange the meeting!"

Proudman held his hands up as the praise band struck the last chord of the song. "Friends, I want to thank you for making this Christmas Eve broadcast a success. And now that the cameras are turned off and the eyes of the world are no longer on us, our family has something we need to share with you, our New Covenant family." Proudman motioned for Angelica and Missy to join him on the platform. Angelica hesitated, but decided that her place was next to Geoffrey. Missy slowly rose, not fully knowing if she could get through the next few minutes. She followed Angelica up the steps and stood on one side of her dad. Angelica stood on the other and Geoffrey wrapped an arm around each of the girls' waists. "About an hour and a half before leaving for the church tonight, we were visited at our home by two Marine officers... two Marines in full dress blue uniforms who brought us the sad and untimely news that our beloved son, Alex, had been killed in action in Afghanistan..." A collective gasp flowed from the crowd, followed by unintelligible murmuring throughout the rows of seats. "We felt it our responsibility, our duty, to honor his selfless sacrifice by following through with this opportunity to reach the world for Christ. So in that spirit I would like to dedicate this service to his memory. Would you pray with and for us?"

"We're with you, Pastor!" Someone shouted from the back of the sanctuary.

"Abba... Father... Merciful God, we give You praise and honor and glory, even in the midst of our pain. We lift up our son, Alex, to You. Receive him into Your loving care and grant him joy and peace and rest from the battle. And for those of us remaining here in the world, we patiently wait for Your peace that passes all understanding to wash over us and lift this sorrow off of our heavy hearts. Take us from this place ready to fight our own battles for the Truth. May we too stand for justice in this world by exhibiting the qualities of He who is above the world. In Christ's name we pray. Amen and amen."

Proudman hugged Angelica and Missy tightly and shepherded them quickly off the back of the platform toward his office, away from the stunned and silent crowd.

chapter

SIX

O daughter of my people, put on sackcloth and roll in ashes; Mourn as for an only son, a lamentation most bitter. For suddenly the destroyer will come upon us.

-Jeremiah 6:26

THE OVAL OFFICE. THE WHITE HOUSE. WASH-INGTON, D.C. - TWO HUNDRED DAYS INTO THE PRESIDENCY OF ANWAR MUHAMMAD ABASI, JR.

"Mr. President, what you're doing is unprecedented in the history of these United States! You can't just terminate nine commanding generals in one fell swoop! You're effectively cut-ting the head off of our military for no good reason. This is a serious breach of national security and a gross violation of protocol!" The Chairman of the Joint Chiefs of Staff, General Marcus E. Dalton, was in a lather. How was he going to coordinate the immediate replacement of nine senior generals? Clearly this president had lost his mind, he thought.

"I want them gone today, General."

"I demand an explanation, Mr. President."

"Demand? You're in no position to demand anything, General. You can do what you are ordered to do, or should we just make it ten generals. Ten's a good round number isn't it?

The Chairman could feel his face flush and his heart rate increase. "Mr. President, I can't very well fire nine generals without so much as an explanation..."

"You'll think of something, General. I have complete faith in you. That'll be all. Thank you."

"But..."

"You are dismissed, General!"

"Very well, Sir." The Chairman spun on his heels and left the Oval Office bewildered. This reckless decision would have great repercussions, he thought as he made his way down the corridor toward the exit. On the list of generals to be fired were General Carter Hamm, United States Army - head of the

United States African Command; Rear Admiral Charles Gaou-
ette, United States Navy – Commander of Carrier Strike Group
Three; Major General Ralph Baker, United States Army – Com-
mander of the Joint Task Force-Horn at Camp Lamar, Djibouti,
Africa; Brigadier General Bryan Roberts, United States Army –
Commander of Fort Jackson and former Commanding Officer
of the 2nd Brigade Combat Team in Iraq; Major General Gregg
A. Sturdevant, United States Marine Corps – Director of Stra-
tegic Planning and Policy for the United States Pacific Com-
mand and Commander of the aviation wing at Camp Bastion,
Afghanistan; Major General Charles M.M. Gurganus, United
States Marine Corps – Regional Commander in the Southwest
and 1st Marine Expeditionary Force, Afghanistan; Lieutenant
General David Holmes Huntoon, Jr., United States Army – 58th
Superintendent of the United States Military Academy at West
Point; Vice Admiral Tim Giardina, United States Navy – Dep-
uty Commander of the United States Strategic Command; and
Major General Michael Carry, United States Air Force – Com-
mander 20th Air Force. Both Giardina and Carry were the top
two commanders in charge of the United States Nuclear Arse-
nal.

General Dalton had asked Abasi for an explanation, but as he
reviewed the list, he knew why these men were chopped. Each of
them had been vocal about and critical of Abasi's policies and lack
of leadership. Each of them had resisted Abasi's directives by ques-
tioning his judgment. And each of them had backbone. Abasi de-
spised men with intestinal fortitude, something completely foreign
to him; and they were patriots, through and through. Abasi knew
they would never go along with his unconstitutional agenda.

Abaddon materialized in the Oval Office, perched on one of the beige sofas set perpendicular to the Resolute Desk. He wasted no time in sharing his irritation with Abasi. "Why are you wasting valuable time with this twit, Dalton? Just pick up the phone and fire the generals yourself. Or better yet, just have them assassinated and be done with it; and while you're at it, kill Dalton... such an imbecile; I want to crush his head like a grape."

"Why the hurry?" Abasi felt he had things well in hand.

"Why the hurry? Why the hurry, you ask? FOOL! Every minute you allow those Christ-followers to remain above ground, another soul is gained for God! The only way to stop the flow into heaven is to kill the Christians who are saving the unsaved. And the only way to kill the Christians is with the military, gutting and burning their churches and cutting off their sanctimonious heads! And the only way to get control of the military is to cut off the heads of the current command structure and replace them with leaders of our choosing, ones sympathetic to our cause... ones we can influence to do our bidding, demonically if necessary. Understand? Do you get the urgency?"

"I understand the strategy and the urgency. It's the implementation that is difficult."

"Nonsense! Kill the generals, all of them, and that numbskull, Dalton. That's why you have the NSA Director in your pocket. Use him and his organization to remove your problematic people. I will arrange for their replacement with suitable minions. Do it!"

Abasi nodded. "But what about public opinion when generals start turning up dead? What will we tell the people?"

"You've been lying to them every day you've been in public office. So, lie to them now. Spin it. Ignore it. Who cares! They will forget all about the generals when you begin ripping the Christians apart. Make the Christians the bad guys. Call them terrorists and hatemongers. Get the gay militants mobilized against them; and the Muslims. Mussies love killing Christians! Use the media and make it open season on hunting down Christians and Jews as enemies of the state. They'll be killing Christ-followers for sport! No one will remember there even were generals! This is going to be such fun!"

Rochelle appeared at the door to the office and she entered without the slightest hesitation. "Master, to what do we owe the pleasure?"

"Rochebel! How is the glamorous life of a First Lady? Hmm? Enjoy abusing the help? Worn out the country's credit card yet?" Abaddon taunted.

Before Rochelle could answer, General Dalton appeared at the office door. "Mr. President, my apologies, but I had to come back. I really must strongly object... oh, forgive me, I didn't realize you had visitors."

"Have a seat, General." Abasi motioned to the sofa across from where Abaddon was sitting.

Dalton moved to the couch and sat down. Abaddon eyed him with open disdain. "I don't believe we've been properly introduced," Dalton rose to shake Abaddon's pasty-white hand.

Abaddon did not reciprocate, but rather chose to ignore Dalton's outstretched hand.

Dalton shrugged. "Forgive me Mr. President. Clearly I have interrupted your meeting. I will come back later."

"Nonsense, General. Have a seat. Relax. This is my father, Lucifer." Abasi smiled while Rochelle moved quietly around the sofa behind Dalton.

Dalton cocked his eyebrow. "Now that's not a name you hear every day."

"Perhaps not," Abasi agreed. "He goes by other names, such as Satan, Abaddon, Father of Lies, Angel of the Abyss, Beelzebub... you get the idea."

Dalton looked perplexed. Rochelle tried to resist, but Jezebel took over inside her, and in one swift motion, reached around Dalton's head with her left hand and clasped tightly on the general's chin. The other hand, she placed firmly on the back of his head and twisted savagely, snapping Dalton's neck like brittle kindling. He collapsed in a heap on the sofa, his head dangling at an odd angle on the back of the couch, his eyes and mouth wide open.

"Now there's a woman who understands the urgency of the situation, Anwar! Maybe the two of you (or is it three of you?) should switch places; she can be president and you can be first lady." Abaddon's amusement was obvious.

"Rochelle! What in the hell...?" Abasi stood with mouth open.

"You have to forgive her," Abaddon chuckled. "She's not herself today."

"But, what do we do with the body? How are we going to dispose of it? You can't just carry a dead general out of the Oval Office, now can you?!" Abasi was in panic mode.

"Oh, ye of little faith," Abaddon waved his hand and he, and the dead Chairman of the Joint Chiefs, vanished.

❧

C.P. Morgan-Proudman and the rest of his ROTC Company at Stephen F. Austin University listened intently as their Company Commander read the latest directive from the Commander in Chief, President Anwar Muhammad Abasi, Jr. "...*effective immediately, all university Army, Air Force, Navy and Marine Corps ROTC cadets will transfer to the newly formed Homeland Security Force (HSF). HSF personnel will take over cadet company command, administrative and training functions immediately. The new HSF curriculum will replace existing curricula immediately..."*

"What in the hell is the Homeland Security Force?" C.P. said under his breath to the cadet seated next to him.

"Beats me," the cadet whispered back.

"...cadets will turn in existing service uniforms and receive HSF uniforms effective immediately..."

"New uniforms? Cool," another cadet whispered.

"Is the HSF gonna have helicopters? I signed up to fly helicopters," C.P. whispered.

"...all existing service contracts are transferred to HSF and new MOS designations will be assigned by an HSF unit administrator according to the needs of the HSF..."

The Company Commander finished reading the directive and placed the order deliberately on the table in front of him. "There you have it ladies and gents. Your Army careers are officially ended, but your career as an HSF officer is about to begin. Your contracts are binding, so there is not much you can do but ride them out. I have been reassigned effective immediately. You will be issued your new uniforms at supply this afternoon and you will meet your new HSF Company Commander at morning formation tomorrow. Don't be late. Any questions?"

C.P. raised his hand.

"Cadet Proudman?"

"Yes, Sir... Sir, is this a good thing?"

"Proudman, you have a knack at cutting right through the horse hockey don't you? But to answer your question, cadet, this whole thing has 'SS' written all over it. I've seen your new uniforms, and let's just say that before the sun sets this evening, people in college towns all over this country are going to be calling you 'Blackshirts.'"

"So, do we have to continue in the program, Sir?" C.P. asked, already sure he knew the answer.

"If you signed a contract, yes. If you haven't signed yet, be prepared to be strong-armed to sign. I've met your new HSF staff; they don't play."

"What would you do, Sir?" C.P.'s question caught the Company Commander off guard.

"Cadet, I've been in this man's Army for more years than I care to remember. I've served two tours in Nam, three tours in Iraq, and I've seen it all. But, in all my years wearing this uniform, I've never seen anything remotely like this... not in America, anyway. If I were you," the Commander paused to choose his words carefully, "...if I were you... if I believed as I know you and I both do... you getting my meaning here, cadet?" C.P. nodded. "...I'd steer as far from the HSF as I possibly could, contract or no contract. People like us won't survive the next 90 days anywhere near a fully activated HSF unit. You copy me, cadet?"

"Yes, Sir, I copy. What will happen if I break the contract, Sir?"

"Son, let me be crystal clear. All of you cadets, hear me well. I've seen the new, so-called, curriculum. I have seen what's coming and it's not good. If you break the contract, the government will consider you a deserter. If you honor the contract, and you profess to be Christian, you will not be allowed to assume a position in the HSF unless you renounce your faith. If you refuse to renounce your faith, you will be considered a terrorist, an enemy of the state, and you will be arrested. Can I make it any clearer?"

"How did this happen, Sir?"

"We fell asleep on our watch, cadet. The enemy got behind our lines and infiltrated every aspect of our lives, and then, little by little, he took control over our media, our government, even our churches. The enemy played on our sense of fairness and equality and we bought into the deception, tolerating everybody and everything in the name of equal rights and diversity, allowing them to borough ever deeper into the fabric of our national identity. And then, when the enemy saw that we had allowed him in to the point of no return, he removed his mask and let us see the horror underneath. And now it's too late to take back all that we have lost."

As the Commander finished his statement, the classroom doors swung open abruptly, and two HSF troopers stepped in, dressed in black shirts with an HSF insignia on a red armband on the left sleeve. The shirts were tucked into khaki trousers, which were bloused atop black leather paratrooper boots. Their heads were covered with a black, baseball cap adorned with the HSF insignia. A black Sam Browne belt, complete with shoulder strap and sidearm holster completed the uniform. The two troopers surveyed the room and then stood to each side of the door, making way for the new HSF Commander to enter. The HSF Commander stepped into the room and looked around with an arrogant, condescending smile. His uniform was similar to the troopers except his trousers were black with a thin red stripe down each leg and he wore a black garrison cover with an HSF insignia on the left side.

"I am Captain Hammad, Commandant of this university's Homeland Security Force company. I know we weren't scheduled to be introduced until morning formation, but I heard you were all assembled already, so I thought we might go ahead and get acquainted. I heard some of the advice your former Company Commander was giving to the young cadet just now, and I have to say that, despite the obvious treasonous tone in his delivery and the whining rant at the end about falling asleep on watch, he is essentially correct. If you want a rewarding career as an HSF officer, it is yours for the taking, provided you complete your curriculum in a satisfactory manner. If you are committed to the outdated notions of the Christian persuasion, you will either renounce those by taking your Oath of Service tomorrow morning or suffer the consequences of your insistence on believing such foolishness. So, I suggest you give it some thought to-night and make a wise choice at tomorrow's formation... yes? So, now you are dismissed to pick up your shiny new uniforms from supply." Captain Hammad turned to one of the HSF troopers and whispered instructions before exiting the classroom.

As the cadets filed out, some were quietly contemplating all they had heard, while others were excitedly discussing the uniforms, seemingly unconcerned about the warning their former CO had just given them. Only a handful, like C.P., Christians and Cadet Martin Werner, the company's only Jew, turned back to the front of the classroom to say goodbye to their Company Commander. Consequently, they were the only ones who witnessed the HSF troopers remove their batons from their belts and beat the Commander to the ground. At first he resisted and fought back, but the sudden intensity of their attack reduced him to covering his head with his hands. Over and over they struck him until his head was bloodied and when he was beyond subdued; they cuffed his wrists and dragged him out of the emergency exit, and threw him into a waiting HSF van. As the van sped off, the remaining cadets watched and wondered if what they had just witnessed was their future as well.

The small remnant of cadets hurried to catch up with the rest of the company at supply to draw their new uniforms, primarily because they had no idea what to do next. Since they were expected to be at supply, C.P. decided that sticking to the program was best, for now, until he had time to think. The others agreed.

C.P.'s walk back to his dorm room was surreal. Carrying his new HSF uniform seemed pointless to him since he knew he would never be able to wear it. Around him, the campus appeared to be functioning as it always had, but he knew that things were not ever going to be the same again. The world would go on, for a time at least; and for those who were in the world, but not of it, things were about to be radically different.

Geoffrey and Simon sat in Geoffrey's office at New Covenant Church, sipping coffee and discussing all things theological. "...I'm simply saying, in the grand design, does God really care about the Augustinian view or the Arminian view when it comes to how we arrive in heaven, because in either case the only way is through the blood of Christ, wouldn't you agree?" Simon asked rhetorically.

Geoffrey nodded, indicating he agreed, but his attention had been caught by the television evening news caption on the wall-mounted flat screen over Simon's shoulder. Geoffrey reached for the remote and pressed the up arrow on the volume control. The volume bar displayed on the screen and as it filled-in from left to right at the bottom of the screen, the announcer gradually became audible: *"The Abasi Administration today issued a series of Executive Orders that are sure to change the way Americans go about their daily routines. For details on this we go to Jonathan Mills, FOX News' White House Correspondent. Jonathan..."*

"President Abasi issued an unprecedented set of Executive Orders today, which his detractors say are unconstitutional. Among the orders issued is E.O. 13759, which creates a new federal paramilitary agency, called the Homeland Security Force, which replaces the existing Homeland Security Agency. The TSA, as well as university ROTC commands, will be a part of this new security force under President Abasi's control. Also issued is E.O. 13760, which mandates all groups on the federal terrorist watch list register with the HSF within the next 90 days. Newly added to the list by the order are all Christian or Jewish clergy. A third executive order, E.O. 13761, appoints HSF monitoring officers to all radio and television broadcasting stations to ensure compliance with federal fairness of information guidelines. And finally, E.O. 13762 makes gathering together in groups of 3 or more for religious purposes, other than the practice of Islam, illegal.

In other government news, President Abasi is restructuring the military, replacing ten commanding generals at once today, including Chairman of the Joint Chiefs of Staff, General Marcus E. Dalton. None of the relieved generals could be found for comment and no details yet on who will be tapped to take those top military posts. I'm Jonathan Mills for FOX News."

"We'll have more news and weather, right after this..."

Geoffrey and Simon sat staring at the screen, even though the news had gone to a commercial. "Was that even real?" Geoffrey said quietly. He hit the menu button on the cable remote to verify which station they were watching and was dismayed to see that it was, in fact, FOX News, and not the Sci-Fi channel.

Simon rubbed his forehead. Suddenly he could feel his heartbeat in his skull and he rubbed his head to eliminate the pressure. "Can he do that?"

"He just did."

"Surely congress will stop him, or even the military... I mean this can't happen here." Simon's disbelief cracked in his voice.

"It's been happening; look at health care. *AbasiCare* was crammed down our throats and then manipulated again and again by executive order to try and make it functional. This move shouldn't surprise me, but this is unprecedented, even for Abasi! He runs on two sets of parallel tracks; he manipulates congress as far as he can push them, and then when he can push them no further, he completes his agenda through executive order. And what in blazes is the HSF? I need to get hold of C.P. at school. If Abasi is converting ROTC units to his personal goon squad, we need to get C.P. out of there A.S.A.P." Proudman still couldn't grasp the enormity of Abasi's decrees. All he knew was that this was bad news. He dialed C.P.'s iPhone, which, of course, went straight to voicemail. "The probability of getting someone's voicemail is directly proportional to the urgency of the call." Proudman shook his head in frustration. He would try again in the morning.

C.P. met Martin Werner at the bottom of the dormitory building stairs the following morning before 0700 formation. Both wore their new HSF Cadet uniforms awkwardly. "There were HSF troopers all around the dorms last night. There was even one patrolling the hallway on my floor," C.P. said quietly as he surveyed the area to make sure nobody was within earshot.

"Mine too." Werner offered.

"Look, I don't know how this is gonna go down; all I know for sure is that I can no more renounce my Christianity than you can your Jewish faith."

"Agreed, but how do we avoid renouncing our faith when it is a condition of the Oath of Service?"

"We don't take the Oath, obviously. We find a way to get past the HSF and off campus while morning formation is going on. Then we get out of Dodge and head for Houston."

"That won't be easy," Martin commented, "especially since they are expecting to see the token Jew renounce his faith this morning. I also notice that there are checkpoints to get on or off campus now. If we don't show up for formation, they will surely be watching for us."

"So we show up for roll call, but leave before the Oath is administered. Just make sure you don't get herded into the front of the formation. Stay toward the back against the building. After roll call we can slide into one of the maintenance doors and make a run for it. If we get separated, meet me at my car in front of the dormitory building."

"It's not much of a plan, but I guess it's all we've got," Werner said nervously.

"It'll work. It's got to. Let's go before we're late and draw attention to ourselves." C.P. slapped Werner on the shoulder and grinned, "It's gonna be okay." As the two cadets double-timed to the courtyard in front of the ROTC building, C.P. wondered if this day would go badly. It had such potential to go wrong, he thought. He prayed for protection and courage. "Lord, please just get me home today."

C.P. and Martin arrived in the courtyard just in time to slide into the last rank of the morning formation. The new HSF Commandant, Captain Hammad, stood on the steps of the ROTC building, watching as the senior cadet began to call roll. No sooner had the cadet started to call the first name, when Captain Hammad stepped forward and placed his hand on the roll sheet, causing the cadet to stop in mid utterance. "Call Cadet Werner forward," he said lowly.

"Cadet Werner, front and center!"

Martin Werner's heart jumped. He could feel his stomach tighten as he fell out of the back rank and walked around the end of the formation to the front. He came to attention in front of the senior cadet and saluted. "Cadet Werner reporting as ordered, Sir."

Captain Hammad brushed the senior cadet aside and stood in front of Werner, who remained at attention. "So, Cadet Werner, you are present and accounted for and all dressed in your HSF uniform."

"Yes, Sir." Werner said quietly.

"So, by that I can surmise that you are prepared to take the Oath of Service, yes?"

"Yes, Sir."

"And, I can also surmise, then, that you are prepared, in taking the Oath, to renounce your Jewish faith, yes?"

"No, Sir."

"Come again, cadet?"

"I said, 'No Sir.'"

"Cadet, the Oath and your renunciation are not mutually exclusive. There cannot be one without the other. Do you understand this?"

"I do, Sir."

"And, are you aware that failure to renounce your Jewish faith is grounds for immediate arrest as an enemy of the state?"

"Yes, I am aware of that, Sir."

"Last chance, Cadet Werner. Do you renounce your faith?"

"No, Sir. I do not."

"Very well, Cadet Werner. Have it your way." Captain Hammad nodded to the HSF troopers on the top of the steps. On cue, they moved in on Cadet Werner, spun him around facing the cadet formation, cuffed him with zip-ties, and kicked the back of his knees, forcing him to kneel at the base of the steps. Captain Hammad removed his sidearm from the holster on his Sam Browne belt and placed the muzzle of his pistol at the back of Werner's head. "Give our regards to your God," he said flippantly as he pulled the trigger. Werner heard the pop just as the lights went out. The formation recoiled, as if one organism, from the sound and the horror. Werner slumped over in the courtyard and a pool of blood formed under his head. HSF troopers moved in to prevent the cadets from breaking formation and running.

C.P.'s head spun from the onslaught to his senses, but he saw the maintenance room door and managed to get inside the door quickly while panic and pandemonium reigned in the courtyard. He pulled his iPhone from his pocket and turned on its flashlight feature. Quickly, he found his way to the maintenance room's interior door and pulled it open. He checked the hallway, and finding it empty, ran down it and up a perpendicular hallway leading to the front of the building. He burst through the double doors and out into the street, running at top speed to the front of his dormitory building where his car was parked. "Got to make it through the checkpoint before they know I'm missing," he said to himself. He started the sporty Scion and fought the urge to speed through campus and risk being pulled over. As he approached the check point, he watched the guards intently. Everything appeared routine, still he prayed silently, "Lord, please just make them wave me through." Two cars ahead of him; now one car ahead of him; now it was his turn and the guard waved him through. He was off campus and on the public road, and he checked his rearview mirror as he accelerated away from the university. "Must get to Hannah... She's in danger; that's the first place they'll look for me."

Angelica opened one eye and looked at the alarm clock. A quarter to eight on a Friday morning. She decided to work from home as the minutes clicked over, one by one, counting down to 7:50 a.m. when her alarm would go off, telling her that she would have to exit her warm, cozy bed. She could smell that Geoffrey had made his coffee, and it motivated her to get up and get a cup of her own. It was only a K-cup away, so she turned off the alarm before its jolting "spaceship-under-attack" siren obliterated the calm.

After stirring her coffee with creamer and three teaspoons of sugar, Angelica found Geoffrey typing away at his laptop in his office. "Good morning," she offered sleepily.

"Mornin', Love. Sleep okay?"

"I guess. Worried about C.P. Did you call again this morning?"

"Not yet."

"I think I'm going to try Hannah to see if she has heard from him this morning."

"Good thought. Shouldn't you be dressed for the office?"

"Working from home today."

"Excellent. Think of it as REALLY casual Friday."

"Exactly." Angelica kissed Geoffrey on the cheek and made her way back to the kitchen counter where she had laid her iPhone. Geoffrey turned his attention back to Sunday's sermon.

Rachel emerged from the guest bedroom dressed in yoga pants and a sweatshirt. Simon followed in a warm-up suit. "Good morning, Angie," Rachel said cheerfully. "We're off for a morning walk. Care to join in?"

"I'd love to, but I'm supposed to be working and I need to take a few minutes to try to reach Hannah, C.P.'s girlfriend at school. We haven't been able to reach C.P. since the news about the HSF taking over ROTC units last night. We just want to know he's okay."

"Make the call, Angie. We'll stay while you do." Simon sat at the kitchen table, motioning Angelica and Rachel to join him.

Angelica pressed Hannah's preset on her phone and put it to her ear. "Hello?" Hannah's raspy, first-word-in-the-morning voice came through.

"Hannah; it's Angelica. I'm so glad you answered. We've been worried about C.P. Have you heard from him this morning?"

"He should be at ROTC already. They were supposed to be meeting their new company commander or something this morning. Is everything okay?"

"I'm sure it is. If you see him, please tell him to check in at home."

"Okay. Bye now."

"Bye." Angelica pressed the END button and shrugged. "She hasn't seen him this morning, but she said that they were meeting the new commander this morning. I can only assume that means the HSF has taken over."

"I'm sure he's fine," Rachel patted Angelica's shoulder.

"I'm sure you're right." Angelica smiled weakly. "Go on, you two. Enjoy that walk."

෮ℳ৹

Abaddon materialized in Hell's War Chamber where Baal was busily overseeing the dispatch of demons for various missions on Earth. His priority, at the moment, was placing a demonically possessed commander and unit at each Homeland Security Force command on every college campus in the United States. These demons would control the students until they could be properly indoctrinated and trained. Additionally, demons were assigned to take possession of any unsaved Secret Service agent currently assigned to Abasi's personal guard. Saved agents were to be reassigned immediately until they could be purged systematically from the agency altogether.

"How long until we are ready to move?" Abaddon questioned his second in command.

"Forty-eight Earth hours at the most, my Lord." Baal answered crisply.

"Excellent, Baal. Excellent. I'm encouraged by your enthusiasm."

"Thank you, my Lord."

"The Christians are in for such a rude awakening. It makes me positively giddy to think of it!"

"Yes, my Lord."

"Carry on then, Baal."

"Yes, my Lord." Baal bowed slightly and resumed giving directions to his commanders.

Abaddon retired to his chambers. He thought of popping in on his son, but then decided he was in far too good a mood to have junior mess it up with his whining and moaning. No, instead he would enjoy the solitude. He reclined on a great stone chaise longue padded with sheep skins and furs, and closed his eyes. It wasn't that he needed sleep, in fact, he could stay awake eternally if he so desired, but rather that he craved rest, which he remembered to be peaceful and calm. He could sleep, but real rest and the refreshment of sleep eluded him. He had not truly rested since God cast him down from heaven. Gabriel had warned him that if he rebelled against God, he would never find peace or rest again. Still he attempted to find them from time to time, retiring to his chambers, reclining on the soft skins, closing his eyes and pushing everything from his mind as best he could. The pursuit of rest was like everything else in his existence: an arrogant, defiant, mad, obsession.

Abaddon's mind wandered as he attempted to chase out anything resembling a cognitive thought. Images of heaven floated by, filling him initially with a sense of melancholy, and then quickly turning to the more familiar hate, envy and despair, which thoughts of his former life usually conjured up. Then, like a video vignette, his fall from the heavenly realm played in his head; driven out by legions of angels, he and his army, spiraling to Earth and then breaking through the mate-

rial bonds to descend into Hell. He recalled the anger and hatred that welled up in him as he fell, shaking a defiant fist at
God as he plummeted downward. He remembered his vow to
curse God and the heavenly host for eternity, and to deceive and
destroy anything and everything God created from that point
forward. Especially mankind. How he hated humans.

His thoughts turned to *The Gathering*. This attempt at
winning souls for Christ irritated him like nothing else; it was
the proverbial thorn in his side. Images of Simon Cross and his
bride, Rachel, taunted him from his dream state. They were so
sickeningly happy together; they were salt to his wounds. And
that insufferable preacher, Geoffrey Proudman and his wife,
Angelica... if the Cross couple burned his memory like salt,
then the Proudman family was a red hot poker to his heart.
Their immeasurable joy was his unspeakable torment. But they
would pay. With Abasi in place and his agenda in motion, the
Christ-followers were about to feel his wrath. His disgusted
sneer turned to a menacing smile as his sleep deepened. He was
gleeful as images of screaming Christians filled his mind, their
blood coating blades of steel wielded by demonic HSF troopers.
He relished the images running chaotically through his brain,
especially the ones where helpless Christians relent and bow to
him in an attempt to save their own lives, only to be killed anyway. He loved the hopeless horror in their faces when they realize that they have given up eternity with God in a moment of
fear and weakness.

The restless demon awoke with a start, peace having eluded him once more. He clutched his head tightly, applying pres-

sure in a vain attempt to slow the frenzied, chaotic thoughts in his head. He staggered to his feet and clutched quill and goatsblood ink from the massive wooden credenza across the chamber. Frantically he dipped the tip of the quill in the blood and scrawled his thoughts on paper in an attempt to purge his head.

Darkest reign consumes the breath
of countless souls condemned to death,
of hopeless, brooding, falling skies
which, dimly light the vanquished eyes
of the lost, the judged and the damned.

Christ's mercy gone and with it rest
beyond the chasm, wide in breadth,
so far from God's eternal light,
absorbed by endless, lifeless night
put away, used up, and wasted.

But rest won't come and grace this night,
for those who long to embrace the light
once more, if it would only be so kind
as to quell this chaos of the mind
that devours, deceives, destroys.

chapter

SEVEN

"Then you will be handed over to be persecuted and put to death, and you will be hated by all nations because of me. At that time many will turn away from the faith and will betray and hate each other, and many false prophets will appear and deceive many people. Because of the increase of wickedness, the love of most will grow cold, but the one who stands firm to the end will be saved. And this gospel of the kingdom will be preached in the whole world as a testimony to all nations, and then the end will come."

-Matthew 24:9-14

As Geoffrey tried in vain to take his mind off C.P.'s whereabouts and well-being, he was relieved to see the white Scion roll into his driveway late Friday afternoon. As he watched from his home office window, C.P. and Hannah exited the vehicle and walked to the back door. Even from his window, Geoffrey could see that they were distressed and Hannah's face was flushed and tear-streaked.

Angelica met them at the back door and hugged them both tightly. C.P. leaned heavily on the granite topped kitchen bar and Hannah sat next to him, perched on a wooden barstool. Neither one spoke.

"We've been trying to reach you for a while now," Angelica said softly. "What's going on?"

Hannah touched C.P.'s shoulder lightly. He looked at Angelica and said calmly, "They killed him. They called his name and he went forward and they shot him in the head because he was a Jew."

"Who shot him? Who did they shoot?"

"The HSF commander. He shot Martin Werner this morning at formation. So I ran. I got out of there; I got Hannah and we drove here. But we couldn't come straight here because all along the main highways they have road blocks and check points looking for ROTC students deserting the HSF because they are Jewish or Christians."

"So why didn't you answer our calls or call us back?"

"We ditched our phones. We didn't want them tracking us by the phones."

"Can they do that?"

"I heard it somewhere. We didn't want to risk it. If they had caught us, they'd have shot us too."

"This can't be happening," Angelica said as Geoffrey entered the kitchen.

"What's the situation out there, Son?" Geoffrey hugged C.P. and then Hannah, grateful they had finally materialized.

"Not good, Dad. They're shooting Jews and Christians in ROTC if they don't renounce their faith to join HSF. And in some cases, they're killing them anyway, even after they do renounce it."

"Are you sure of this?" Geoffrey felt compelled to ask even though he could see C.P.'s forthrightness and truthful intensity.

"They shot Cadet Werner right in front of the whole company of cadets, Dad! He wouldn't renounce his faith and they killed him for it! Then, on the way here, we had to take back roads, because when we hit the traffic lined up at the first road block outside Nacogdoches, we saw them pull several cadets from their cars. They put them on their knees on the side of the road and executed them right there! We turned around and took county roads all the way here."

Hannah sat at the kitchen table and shivered. "When I woke up this morning, my biggest worry was turning in my creative writing paper on time. Now I can't even go back to school because of the HSF. It's only a matter of time before they start looking for Christians everywhere on campus, not just the ROTC. How did this happen? Why are they doing this? Can't someone stop this?"

Simon had entered the kitchen during Hannah's recounting of the day's events. "The problem, my dear girl, is that there is no one to report this to who can be trusted. If the HSF is evil, who's to say the Sheriff's Department or the State Troopers or the County Constables aren't also in collaboration with them?"

"What are we to do?" Angelica asked nobody in particular.

"I say we shelter in place for now and try to gather information via the internet. Broadcast news will be compromised, I'm sure. It wouldn't hurt to make a trip to the grocery store for non-perishables before the word gets out and there's a run on the stores. Simon and I will go. Angelica... you, Rachel, Missy, Freddie, Hannah and C.P. stay here and stay watchful. Also, get the propane company on the phone and get them to come out and fill up the tank. Who knows how long we will have ordinary services." Proudman looked at all the faces around him to see if there were questions. "Okay. Let's go." As he gathered his keys and his wallet, Proudman pulled Angelica to the side. "Your pistol is loaded and in the nightstand by the bed. The shotgun is loaded and in our closet by my dresser. Just in case."

Angelica nodded.

⟡

President Abasi assembled his new array of military advisors and the new head of the Homeland Security Forces, General Qassim Suleimani, in the War Room, far below the White House. Suleimani, formerly the shadowy commander of Iran's paramilitary (read terrorist) Quds Force, was now the United States' most powerful military commander. Although technically subordinate to the Chairman of the Joint Chiefs of Staff, the new puppet chairman knew better than to get in Suleimani's way. The HSF was Abasi's muscle, and every service commander knew that they were just a bullet-in-the-dark away from being replaced at any given moment.

"Gentlemen, the time has come to eradicate the enemies of the state that have been chewing the fabric of civilized society, fraying its delicate edges and causing the tapestry to unravel, bit by bit." Abasi paced around the conference table as he spoke. "For too long the Jews and Christ-lovers have perpetrated their hate crimes against Americans, pushing their Judeo-Christian filth on society, demanding that everyone adhere to archaic values that rob citizens of their right to be individual, equal, and diverse. Equality is, after all, what this nation was founded on, right?"

"Yes, Mr. President!"

"So, Sunday morning, as the Christ-followers assemble to worship their God, we will descend on them systematically in every major city, crushing their will to gather in churches from this day forward."

"Mr. President, how can we possibly have enough manpower to shut down every church in this country? There must be hundreds of thousands of them." The new Commanding General of the Army spoke up from his seat at the conference table.

"General, er... Qatar, is it?"

"Yes, Mr. President."

"General Qatar, we don't have to enter every single church to shut them all down. If we hit the major churches in the major cities, the fear will spread as fast as the news will carry it, and the Sunday after, most churches will not convene out of sheer terror!" Abasi slammed his fist on the table next to Qatar to emphasize his point. "Then we will begin hunting the individual Christ-followers and Jews until not one, man, woman or child remains. And then, we will turn our vast military might on Israel and the rest of the world, until one by one, we will bring about the New World Order!"

"For Allah!" One of Abasi's generals shouted in the heat of the moment.

"Yes... yes, for Allah," Abasi continued the deception.

"Brilliant, Mr. President," Qatar groveled his approval.

"Gentlemen, I want you to take your direction from General Suleimani for this operation. He is acting under my direct authority as Commander in Chief, so his orders are my orders. Understand?"

"Yes, Mr. President."

"Excellent. And so it begins, gentlemen. The purging of our nation. The end of more than two centuries of Judeo-Christian oppression. *Allahu Akbar! Allahu Akbar! Allahu Akbar!*"

"Allahu Akbar! Allahu Akbar! Allahu Akbar!" The room erupted in chanting as Abasi's generals climbed on board the Islamo-fascist juggernaut. Abasi smiled. "How convenient is the Muslim hatred," he thought to himself.

Geoffrey was up and around much earlier than usual this Sunday morning; the storm from the night before had subsided in the witching hour, and Geoffrey took the watch from Simon around 2:00 a.m. The watch was precautionary, but prudent given the circumstances described by C.P. and Hannah regarding their difficult trek home from Nacogdoches. There was no knowing what the HSF was capable of at this point. Would they go to the lengths required to track down AWOL personnel at their home of record? Was C.P. in danger if he remained at home? Was the entire family in danger by association? Certainly Proudman was on the watch list as a pastor. There was so much uncertainty.

But one thing was certain in Proudman's mind: After the long Friday and Saturday nights of watching and wondering they had just endured, Church was going on as scheduled this Sunday morning. Proudman picked up his sermon notes and scanned through them, already convicted by the Holy Spirit that the message had changed. The circumstances dictated that a new message be preached; but what message? There was no time to write a whole new sermon, but Proudman had been here before. He knew that the words would come. So, instead of racking his brain trying to discern the new message, Geoffrey decided to simply go to his knees in prayer.

"Abba, Father, I am powerless to influence my congregation without Your Word flowing through me and out of me. Father, there is most assuredly a storm coming. I know that it can no longer be avoided. But I also know that You promised to be with Your people through the storms, so I claim that promise now. Give me the words of explanation, the words of comfort, the words of direction and guidance to bring Your people at New Covenant Church safely to the shore. And, Abba, Father, protect them in the coming days so that they are delivered from evil in all its forms. And keep them steadfast in their faith, so that they make wise choices that are pleasing and honoring to You. I pray all these things in the mighty, everlasting name of Jesus. Amen."

As Geoffrey had done on countless Sunday mornings before, he went to the kitchen and made a cup of coffee for Angelica, three spoons full of sugar with half-and-half, and brought it to her bedside table. He gently kissed her forehead and softly wished her, "Good morning, Babe," as her eyes flickered open.

"Are we going to church? Is that wise?" Angelica asked sleepily.

"It's what we are called to do; now more than ever," Geoffrey replied gently.

Angelica nodded. That was good enough for her; she was all in. She hit the remote to raise the head of the bed so that she could stay under the warm covers and sip her coffee. She picked up the television remote and pressed the power button, hoping to catch a weather report. Instead there was a talking head analyzing Sunday morning alternatives for former church goers. Now that it wasn't fashionable, prudent or legal to be seen at church, the government was helping people choose more politically correct activities to fill one's Sunday morning. Angelica flipped the channel in disgust and continued until she found a weather report. Cool and breezy. No chance of rain in the forecast.

As was his routine, Geoffrey went in to Missy's room and woke her gently to give her first opportunity to hit the showers before anyone else got to them. She needed extra time to get ready most mornings, and for some reason her brothers had not ever grasped the concept of a "quick" shower. Next he opened Freddie's door and slid his hand over the light switch, turning on the overheads. "Reveille, sports fan!" Freddie squinted and pulled his pillow over his face. Geoffrey then opened C.P.'s door, flipped on the lights and greeted him with a "Rise and shine,

Valentine!" in his best drill instructor voice. C.P. responded in usual fashion by pulling the covers over his head. Then, remembering to add Hannah to his wake up roster, Geoffrey knocked gently on the guest bedroom door.

"I'm awake," was all he needed to hear from inside the room and Geoffrey padded back to the kitchen to ensure coffee was made for Simon and Rachel. Church was happening this morning, and the Proudman household was in motion to make sure that it did.

The Reverend Geoffrey Proudman was floored when he walked out on to the platform at New Covenant Church for the early service. He looked out over the auditorium and every single seat was filled. There were people everywhere, not just members, but new people who had never been to New Covenant before. The aisles were full of people sitting on the floor, as was the open area between the platform and the first row of seats. All the floor space in the wings was full of people and there were people standing along the side walls and the back wall of the sanctuary. The balcony was full and people were sitting on the stairs that served as the aisles for the balcony seats. Proudman estimated there were close to two thousand, easily doubling the size of the regular membership.

Angelica had taken her usual seat along with Simon, Rachel and the rest of the Proudman family, plus Hannah. They too were astounded by the unprecedented turnout. The atmosphere was intense; a mixture of expectation and apprehension, of hope and fear.

Proudman walked to the podium and motioned for the praise team to take their seats. The air was filled with a sense of urgency, and Proudman decided to begin his sermon immediately and not go through the normal flow of worship. He took a swallow of water from the glass on the podium and began his message.

"It is not by accident that every square inch of space is occupied in this sanctuary this morning. No doubt the events of the past few days have driven many of you here, perhaps to a church for the very first time in your lives. If you were compelled to show up here, especially in the face of impending persecution and the threat of death, then you can be sure that you have been called by God. Now I know that many of you here this morning have a relationship with Jesus Christ. And I also know that just as many of you out there have no clue what that means. But, I'm here to tell you, 'that's okay.' I'm here to tell you that you are welcome here and that by the time you leave here this morning; you will at least know what steps you must take to begin a relationship with Jesus. I'm also here to tell you this morning that you are out of time, so don't waste precious minutes mulling things over... it's now or never.

While the persecution of Christians in this country to the magnitude we are experiencing today may have caught you off guard, I can tell you that if you have spent any time reading a Bible, you should have seen it coming. In John's gospel account,

Jesus says, *'If the world hates you, you know that it has hated Me before it hated you. If you were of the world, the world would love its own; but because you are not of the world, but I chose you out of the world, because of this the world hates you. Remember the word that I said to you, 'A slave is not greater than his master.' If they persecuted Me, they will also persecute you; if they kept My word, they will keep yours also. But all these things they will do to you for My name's sake, because they do not know the One who sent Me.'* (John 15:18-21)

The world despises us because we stand for Jesus. And Jesus stands for God the Father. And God stands for Principle, Mind, Soul, Spirit, Life, Truth and Love. The world stands for the elevated human, rather than the Risen Christ. The world stands for tolerance, diversity and universalism, rather than righteousness, holiness and perfect justice. The world stands for all things anti-Christ, rather than a Christ who is all in all!

In 2 Timothy Paul says, *'But realize this, that in the last days difficult times will come. For men will be lovers of self, lovers of money, boastful, arrogant, revilers, disobedient to parents, ungrateful, unholy, unloving, irreconcilable, malicious gossips, without self-control, brutal, haters of good, treacherous, reckless, conceited, lovers of pleasure rather than lovers of God, holding to a form of godliness, although they have denied its power; Avoid such men as these.'* (2 Timothy 3:1-5)

Do any of those character traits sound like someone you know? Do they accurately portray most of the people you know who shout out venomously against anyone who speaks against gay marriage? Do those character traits resemble all those who attack anyone who dares to stand up for the rights of the unborn? Do these traits mark the godly, or are they the mark of the ungodly world beyond these sanctuary walls?

'Now you followed my teaching, conduct, purpose, faith, patience, love, perseverance, persecutions, and sufferings, such as happened to me at Antioch, at Iconium and at Lystra; what persecutions I endured, and out of them all the Lord rescued me! Indeed, all who desire to live godly in Christ Jesus will be persecuted. But evil men and impostors will proceed from bad to worse, deceiving and being deceived. You, however, continue in the things you have learned and become convinced of, knowing from whom you have learned them...' (2 Timothy 3:10-14)

Jesus knew that we, the Church, would be persecuted for His name's sake; and He told us so in no uncertain terms. We are a threat to the New World Order, the order of secular humanist society, the order of the atheist, the agnostic and the anti-Christ. And even those that profess not to believe are only deceiving themselves by denying a basic and universal truth: that God exists and that He is sovereign. In John 12:42-44 it is written, *'Nevertheless many even of the rulers believed in Him, but because of the Pharisees they were not confessing Him, for fear that they would be put out of the synagogue; for they loved the approval of men rather than the approval of God. And Jesus cried out and said, "He who believes in Me, does not believe in Me but in Him who sent Me."'*

So what do we do with the knowledge that we as Christ-followers are due to be persecuted? If you are on the fence about a decision for Jesus, or if you are a new Christian, that's got to be sobering news. And, even if you have been on this journey for a while, you may be wondering why you signed up for this privilege of persecution. Fortunately, beloved, Jesus gives us the answer to that question. In Matthew, Jesus says, *'Behold, I send you out as sheep in the midst of wolves; so be shrewd as serpents and innocent as doves. But beware of men, for they will hand you over to the courts and scourge you in their synagogues; and you will even be brought before governors and kings for My sake, as a testimony to them and to the Gentiles. But when they hand you over, do not worry about how or what you are to say; for it will be given you in that hour what you are to say. For it is not you who speak, but it is the Spirit of your Father who speaks in you.'* (Matthew 10:16-20)

You see, beloved, you are a living testimony to the world, to the everyday people and to the rulers, a living testimony for Christ! Yes, they will persecute you and abuse you and scoff at you, but do not worry because the Holy Spirit of God will give you the words to speak when the time comes!

'Why, Pastor? Why would we do this? Why would we put ourselves in harm's way just to tell the story of Jesus and His gift of salvation?' An excellent question! And for that question too, Jesus has the answer. Jesus said, *'Blessed are those who have been persecuted for the sake of righteousness, for theirs is the kingdom of heaven. Blessed are you when people insult you and persecute you, and falsely say all kinds of evil against you because of Me. Rejoice and be glad, for your reward in heaven is great; for in the same way they persecuted the prophets who were before you.'* (Matthew 5:10-12)

Did you get that? Do you see it? We do this because our reward in heaven is great! We can rejoice and be glad in the midst of our persecution. When we stand up for Christ, when we do

what is right, what we have been called and commanded to do...
God rewards that action in heaven! Still need more motivation?
Then consider what Paul says in Romans 8:16-18. He says, *'The
Spirit Himself testifies with our spirit that we are children of God, and
if children, heirs also, heirs of God and fellow heirs with Christ, if in-
deed we suffer with Him so that we may also be glorified with Him.
For I consider that the sufferings of this present time are not worthy to
be compared with the glory that is to be revealed to us.'*

I don't know about you, beloved, but I want to be an heir!
The promise is that this momentary light affliction is producing for us an eternal weight of glory! That's 2 Corinthians 4:17
in case you want to refer to that passage later. In fact, no, let's
look at it together, Church, because it's just too good to pass
up. Paul says in 2 Corinthians 4:16-18, *'Therefore we do not lose
heart, but though our outer man is decaying, yet our inner man is being
renewed day by day. For momentary, light affliction is producing for
us an eternal weight of glory far beyond all comparison, while we look
not at the things which are seen, but at the things which are not seen; for
the things which are seen are temporal, but the things which are not seen
are eternal.'*

Beloved, the persecution is temporary; the reward is forever. I'll say that again... the persecution is temporary; the reward
is forever. Hear me now, Church, and here me well... my son,
Christian Peter, narrowly escaped execution at the hands of his
HSF Commander this past Friday morning. He and his company of cadets watched helplessly as one of their fellow cadets,
Cadet Martin Werner, was brutally and summarily executed in
front of the morning formation for no other reason than he was

Jewish and refused to renounce his faith. The same scenario has been carried out on university campuses all across the land, with Jews and Christians mercilessly gunned down, martyred for their faith in God. This is the New World Order. This is Abasi's America. And make no mistake… now that Abasi has his shock troops in place, the individual Christian is Abasi's next target. You and I, and those we love, are in the government's crosshairs. Will we renounce our faith and live a short while longer, or will we stand for Christ and live forever with Him?

Mark's gospel says, *'And when he had called the people unto him with his disciples also, he said unto them, Whosoever will come after me, let him deny himself, and take up his cross, and follow me. For whosoever will save his life shall lose it; but whosoever shall lose his life for my sake and the gospel's, the same shall save it. For what shall it profit a man, if he shall gain the whole world, and lose his own soul?'* (Mark 8:34-36)

Beloved, the day of our persecution is upon us. And death may be on our doorstep this very moment. But be not afraid! *'Fear not the things which thou art about to suffer: behold, the devil is about to cast some of you into prison, that ye may be tried; and ye shall have tribulation ten days. Be thou faithful unto death, and I will give thee the crown of life. He that hath an ear, let him hear what the Spirit saith to the churches. He that overcometh shall not be hurt of the second death.'* (Revelation 2:10-11)

This is a difficult message for difficult times. But you know the Truth. You know whose you are. So for those hearing the invitation to come to Christ and be spared the bondage of this dark world, bow your heads and say this prayer with me, 'Abba, Father, I am weak. I am a sinner in need of a Savior. Extend to me Your mercy and grace through the blood of Your only be-gotten Son, Jesus Christ. Lord Jesus, I confess that I have lived a sinful life and I am helpless to extract myself from sin of my own power. I ask You to come into my heart and to be my Lord and my Savior. By the power of Your Name, I claim Your saving grace because You died for my sins on the cross, and then rose from the grave, shattering the hold of death on all those who call You Lord and believe on You for their salvation. I love you Jesus, and I make You Lord of my life. Amen.'"

Proudman could feel the urging of the Holy Spirit. He knew time had run out even before he heard the steady beat of rotor blades descending on the church grounds. "Listen to me, Church. There is no time left. If you prayed that prayer and you invited Jesus into your heart, rest assured that you have been born again. I know you haven't had time to even scratch the sur-face of your new relationship with Christ, so I will just give you this to hold onto through the trial you are about to endure... keep your eyes on Him and never look away. No matter what comes at you, keep your eyes on Jesus and never deny Him for anything, not even the promise of your own life. Remember that. Never forget. Blessed be the Name of the Lord."

Just as Proudman finished his sentence, the doors to the sanctuary burst open and an entire squad of HSF troopers stormed in. Those people in and closest to the aisles were greet-ed with rifle butts to the head and torso, causing the congrega-tion to erupt in panic. Some tried to break past the troopers and were shot in mid-stride. Others tried to run down the aisles toward the platform, stepping on those who were already seated in the aisles, but they received bullets in their backs for their trouble and fell, dead or dying and bleeding, onto their fellow parishioners. The remaining people dropped to the floor between the rows of seats and tried to avoid being shot. Mothers held their kids tightly, while fathers tried to shield their families with their own bodies. The gunfire was deafening and the sounds of bullets impacting seats, walls and bodies caused everyone to press themselves into the floor.

The squad of HSF troopers deployed through the sanctuary, covering every possible escape route, and pointed their weapons threateningly at the crowd. The din of gunshots subsided, and through it emerged the groans and screams of the injured and dying, and the sobs and whimpers of frightened mothers and children. Angelica clutched Missy, Hannah and Rachel, while Simon held back an overzealous C.P. from a fruitless attempt to attack the closest HSF trooper. Freddie placed himself between the HSF troopers and the women and gritted his teeth, wondering how none of the many bullets impacting near him had his name on it. After a few moments of intense fear and uncertainty, the HSF Commander from Stephen F. Austin University, Captain Hammad, entered through the sanctuary doors. He walked down the aisle, an HSF trooper ahead of him kicking and rifle-butting people out of the way, clearing a path to the platform where Proudman stood.

Hammad picked up the wireless microphone from the podium and stood next to Proudman. The accompanying trooper nudged Proudman with his rifle barrel, indicating that he should kneel. "Hands behind your head," the trooper ordered. Proudman complied.

Hammad eyed the crowd with a smirk across his thin lips. His middle-eastern accent jarred the congregation's sensibilities as he began to speak. "I am Captain Hammad, Commandant of the Stephen F. Austin University unit of the Homeland Security Force. I am here in pursuit of a deserter believed to be a member of this church. And, since I have your attention, you may as well know that, by order of His Excellency, President Abasi, you are unlawfully assembled for an illegal religious purpose, specifically the practice of Christianity. You are all enemies of the state and are now under arrest. Any resistance will be dealt with harshly. You will be taken from here by bus to a processing center where you will undergo re-education and will be given the opportunity to renounce your faith and return to your homes. I think you will find it to be an agreeable choice compared to the alternative. Those of you wishing to convert to the state-sanctioned religion, Islam, may do so at that time; in fact I highly recommend it."

Proudman shifted his weight from his knees to his haunches and the movement brought Hammad's attention to him once again. Hammad was obvious in his enjoyment of his new role as HSF thug. He brought the microphone up to his mouth once again and began to gloat over the kneeling preacher. "So, Reverend, where is your God now? It seems to me the only one with the power to save you in this auditorium is me." Hammad removed his pistol from its holster. C.P. had seen this scene before and the outcome had not been good for Cadet Werner. Simon worked to restrain C.P. as Hammad continued, "Tell all of these good people that you are choosing life over your Christ, Reverend. Renounce your faith and I will let you go home with your family this morning." Hammad put the microphone in front of Proudman's face.

Geoffrey looked around the sanctuary at all of the faces looking back at him. Many he knew well; many he didn't know at all. He looked at his Angelica, who stood below the platform looking up at him with tears streaming down her face. He looked at Missy, who had already endured so much in her relatively short faith-walk. He looked at C.P. who was straining against Simon to take action... any action. He looked at Freddie, still shielding the women as best he could with his own body. "When had he become such a man?" Proudman thought. And he looked at his dear friends, Simon and Rachel and he remembered all they had been through together as it flashed through his mind like a video on ultra-fast reverse. It seemed an eternity since *The Gathering*. The trooper behind him nudged him with his rifle barrel. Proudman began to speak, clearly and succinctly, "You want me to choose life over Christ; but I say to you today, in front of all of these witnesses, CHRIST IS LIFE! There is no other choice. What you do here this morning is of no consequence."

As Proudman spoke, the congregation erupted in cheers and shouts of "AMEN!" and "HALLELULIA!" The troopers rifle-butted a few people close to them in an attempt to regain control of the crowd, but they would not be silenced.

Hammad, fuming, lowered his pistol at the back of Proudman's skull. Angelica's eyes locked with her husband's, and in an instant she made a desperate choice. In the midst of the pandemonium, she bolted past Freddie for the platform steps. Simon, seeing her move, released C.P. from his grip, and he shot like a bolt from a crossbow toward the closest trooper. Proudman responded with years of hand-to-hand combat training as the trooper behind him raised his weapon to repel Angelica's advance up the platform steps. Geoffrey reached above his head and grasped the end of the trooper's rifle barrel, pulling him forward and off balance. With the other hand, Proudman grasped the trooper's rifle stock and jammed it full force into the trooper's lower jaw, shattering it and causing him to collapse in a heap below the platform. At the same time, Angelica reached Hammad and drove the butt of her hand into the Commander's throat, dropping him to his knees. He dropped the microphone and clutched his throat, while Angelica kicked the pistol from his other hand. Hammad coughed violently, spewing blood. He collapsed on the platform choking on his crushed windpipe. Proudman grabbed the pistol and spun around in time to see C.P. land a knockout blow to the nearest trooper. Proudman quickly sighted in on the next closest trooper and drilled two rounds into his chest, killing him instantly. Simon took out a fourth trooper with a punch to the face, relieving the trooper of his weapon. Proudman motioned for Missy, Freddie, Hannah and Rachel to run for the exit behind the platform. C.P. collected the rifle from the trooper he had downed; he and Simon made their way quickly to the exit behind Freddie and the girls. The congregation bolted for every available exit all at once, overwhelming and trampling the remaining HSF troopers, who lost heart at the sight of their fallen commander and comrades. Proudman nodded approvingly at Angelica and fired two rounds into Hammad for good measure. Angelica raised an eyebrow at him and he shrugged. The couple then moved quickly toward the exit behind the others.

The Proudman family, with Hannah, Simon and Rachel, rendezvoused at the church van and Geoffrey hit the remote to unlock the doors. He jumped into the driver's seat and the rest of the crew piled in. "Are we all here?"

Angelica counted, "Missy, Freddie, C.P., Hannah, Simon, Rachel and you and me. Check! All here!"

Geoffrey gunned the motor and the van lurched forward and joined the mass exodus of church goers out of the parking lot and away from the church. "We'll head for the house and make a plan," Proudman said. "We won't want to stay there long. I'm sure the HSF will descend on us as soon as they figure out what's happened."

"Indeed." Simon agreed.

The Reverend Proudman wondered how many of his congregation had been lost. So many bullets. So much chaos. So much blood. He wanted to go back and tend to the dying and injured. He wanted to count his dead and mourn for them properly. But he knew that was impossible now. This Sunday marked the start of a new season of persecution and horror for the Church. Proudman knew that things were going to be radically different from this moment forward. "Come quickly, Lord Jesus," was all he could manage to pray.

cⅤɔ

President Abasi sat in the War Room with General Qassim Suleimani, watching satellite and drone images come in
from around the country as the Homeland Security Forces con-
ducted their Sunday morning purge of congregating Christians.
Some of the commanders in the field had live feeds and embed-
ded media accompanying them as they raided churches, slaughtered pastors, priests and deacons and rounded up whole con-
gregations to be sent to re-education camps. Abasi was giddy as
GoPro cameras mounted on HSF commanders and government
media personnel showed, in high-resolution detail, the brutal
attacks on innocent church-goers.

The re-education camps were hastily built, many of
them from former FEMA sites. These were stark, but functional institutions of plain white trailers, converted to serve
as barracks, ringed with hurricane fencing topped with con-
certina wire. Each camp could accommodate several thousand prisoners. The administration offices, kitchen, and stor-
age warehouse were in the center of the compound, and were
each made of prefabricated metal buildings. Also central to
each camp was a large open area used for formations, exercise
and punishment. In the center of the large open area was a
poured concrete pad, large enough to hold a six-foot by three-
foot wooden altar. Next to that, set into the slab on one end
of the altar, was a thick, wooden post on which was mounted
shackles and chains, in such a position as to bind a person's
hands high above their head. A portable guillotine stood eight
feet tall on the opposite end of the altar. The unit was trailer-

mounted, light-weight and could be towed by almost any vehicle with a hitch. And next to the concrete pad, an eight-foot high, twelve-foot long concrete wall faced the open field. The wall served as a suitable backstop for firing squads. By design, a second concrete pad was set on the other end of the backstop wall, so that the wall was nestled between the two pads. While the first pad was for punishment, torture and execution, the second pad was for re-education. On this pad was a large, pole-mounted photo of President Abasi, a 90-inch wide-screen television and a sign on which was written the Shahada, *"There is no god but Allah, and Muhammad is Allah's prophet."* The placement of the pads sent a clear visual message to the prisoners: conform and convert to the state-sanctioned religion of Islam, or suffer agonizing torture and death.

All across the country, the camps were filling up as church after church fell to the systematic HSF invasion. "I wish my father could see this," Abasi said gleefully.

"I am seeing this," Abaddon said as he manifested in the War Room. Demon-possessed Secret Service men genuflected at their master's arrival.

"Father! Welcome! Look," Abasi said, pointing to the bank of screens, each with a different feed showing Christians beaten, shot and herded into camps like cattle.

"Magnificent!" Abaddon gushed approvingly. "Well done!"

General Suleimani sat with his mouth open in obvious shock and confusion at Abaddon's sudden manifestation. Abasi noticed. "General, where are my manners? This is my father, Abaddon."

"As-salaam alaykum," Suleimani offered greetings.

"Wa 'alaykum al-salaam," Abaddon responded with amusement.

Suleimani searched for something else to say in the awkward silence after Abaddon's returned greeting. "Allah be praised for your son and his mission to rid the world of the infidels! And thanks to Muhammad, peace be upon him, for his revelation of Islam!"

Abaddon chuckled. "Rid the world of the infidels. How very amusing, General. I gave you Allah. Your people were worshiping inanimate objects, rocks, stars and moons until I purchased your prophet's soul for a few years of power and a couple of adolescent boys."

"I... don't understand..." Suleimani muttered.

"Allah is an ancient pagan moon-god, my gullible friend. Thousands and tens of thousands like you are boiling and toiling away in the Abyss right this very moment because they bought into Muhammad's lie, a lie of my invention; a lie called

Islam. Haha! Brilliant!" Abaddon's chuckle turned to outright laughter. Abasi joined in, clutching his gut, as he found his father's revelation to the general quite amusing.

"But, then, what has become of the prophet? Surely he is in paradise with his multitude of virgins!" Suleimani protested.

Abaddon nearly fell over at the general's protest. "Ahh-HaHaHa! Virgins! Hahahaha! There are many women in Hell, General, but I assure you... none of them are virgins! And I can further attest, your prophet, Muhammad, has...'other appetites.' Hahahaha!" Abaddon was thoroughly amused. Abasi grinned like a school boy. Suleimani sulked in his chair.

chapter

EIGHT

"Do not let your heart be troubled; believe in God, believe also in Me. In My Father's house are many dwelling places; if it were not so, I would have told you; for I go to prepare a place for you. If I go and prepare a place for you, I will come again and receive you to Myself, that where I am, there you may be also."

-John 14:1-3

Geoffrey Proudman and crew rolled into their home driveway in the church van. Proudman was glad they had not ever gotten around to putting the New Covenant Church logo on the van's exterior. The plain white van was much less conspicuous.

"Okay people, we don't have much time here. Pack light. One bag each with sensible clothes. We should grab bottled water and non-perishables. Also firearms and ammo, the toolbox from the garage, flashlights with batteries, the first aid kit from the kitchen pantry and wallets, purses and the like. Our next stop is the bank. We need cash, so we should withdraw as much as possible. We leave here in 20 minutes or less, so move!"

The crew dismounted and set about accomplishing all that Geoffrey had directed. Simon and Geoffrey went to the garage to get the water, tools and batteries. "Where do we go from here," Simon asked as he gathered essential tools from the workbench and tossed them in a gray metal toolbox.

"Angelica and I bought a small place in the hill country a while back, right after we returned from Israel. It's on about 50 acres of rolling countryside. It was our weekend getaway, and we thought someday we would settle there to enjoy our declining years. We've been fixing it up on Saturdays and holidays. It's away from the beaten path and situated on high ground; you can see someone coming for miles."

"Sounds like a good place to be."

"It will be a good place to regroup and try to determine what's next for us."

"Do these events strike you as tribulation events?" Simon asked.

"Well, because of my studies, I'm prone to believe that the tribulation occurs after the rapture of the Church. I'm also of the mind that the Holy Spirit is still at work in the world, which further indicates that we are not in the tribulation period yet. But, recent events certainly suggest we are close... very close. No person knows when Christ will return to gather His Church, but it can't happen soon enough for me." Proudman put fresh batteries into a flashlight as he spoke.

"Indeed; But, what are the scriptural reference points that describe the rapture of the Church?"

Geoffrey picked up a Bible from the workbench and opened it. "Well, my learned friend, Matthew 24 says, '*And then the sign of the Son of Man will appear in the sky, and then all the tribes of the earth will mourn, and they will see the Son of Man coming on the clouds of the sky with power and great glory. And He will send forth His angels with a great trumpet and they will gather together His elect from the four winds, from one end of the sky to the other.*

Now learn the parable from the fig tree: when its branch has already become tender and puts forth its leaves, you know that summer is near; so, you too, when you see all these things, recognize that He is near, right at the door. Truly I say to you, this generation will not pass away until all these things take place. Heaven and earth will pass away, but My words will not pass away.

But of that day and hour no one knows, not even the angels of heaven, nor the Son, but the Father alone.' In other words, you will know that the time is approaching as the signs of the time become clear."

"Understandable." Simon picked up a tire patch kit off of the workbench and tossed it into the toolbox.

"Matthew goes on, in Chapter 24, to give us simple scenarios so that we understand the suddenness with which Christ will come. He writes, *'Then there will be two men in the field; one will be taken and one will be left. Two women will be grinding at the mill; one will be taken and one will be left.'*"

Simon nodded and responded, "So one of these days, you and I will simply vanish off the face of the Earth and leave the unsaved behind to deal with the tribulation." Cross loved discussing Christ's return; Christ's promise to return always gave him such incredible hope for the future especially in these trying days.

"That's right! Jesus told his disciples he would return for them, and for us, in John 14. He told them, *'Do not let your heart be troubled; believe in God, believe also in Me. In My Father's house are many dwelling places; if it were not so, I would have told you; for I go to prepare a place for you. If I go and prepare a place for you, I will come again and receive you to Myself, that where I am, there you may be also.'* Can you imagine, Simon, that if Christ Himself has been preparing a place for us for all this time, what a magnificent place that must be?"

"Indeed." Simon allowed his mind to wander into that place of God's promise. What would his dwelling place look like? Simon appreciated magnificent places; he had seen many marvelous sights in his travels, breathtaking views, incredible structures, palaces, and royal gardens. But for all of their majesty and beauty, Simon knew they would pale in comparison to what Jesus had waiting for him.

"In Acts, I think it's the first chapter, it says, *'And after He had said these things, He was lifted up while they were looking on, and a cloud received Him out of their sight. And as they were gazing intently into the sky while He was going, behold, two men in white clothing stood beside them. They also said, "Men of Galilee, why do you stand looking into the sky? This Jesus, who has been taken up from you into heaven, will come in just the same way as you have watched Him go into heaven.'* Christ's ascension into heaven left the disciples dazed and confused until God's messengers showed up to bring them back on point. The angels confirmed His return to Earth; back the same way He left! And in 1 Corinthians 15, Paul tells us that some of us will be living and breathing when Christ returns. He writes, *'Behold, I tell you a mystery; we will not all sleep, but we will all be changed, in a moment, in the twinkling of an eye, at the last trumpet; for the trumpet will sound, and the dead will be raised imperishable, and we will be changed.'* This also describes what happens to those believers who have already died. They will rise first and be restored to their glorified bodies, and then those living will be transformed into their glorified bodies. And, all of that occurs when the trumpet sounds. Won't that be a sound for sore ears!

Paul reconfirms this in his first letter to the Thessalonians. There he writes, *'For the Lord Himself will descend from heaven with a shout, with the voice of the archangel and with the trumpet of*

God, and the dead in Christ will rise first. Then we who are alive and remain will be caught up together with them in the clouds to meet the Lord in the air, and so we shall always be with the Lord.'"

"Glorified bodies," Simon mused. "Fascinating."

"Oh, yes. You can't go traipsing around heaven in these old ragged bodies. In fact Paul says in Philippians, Chapter 3, I recall, *'For our citizenship is in heaven, from which also we eagerly wait for a Savior, the Lord Jesus Christ; who will transform the body of our humble state into conformity with the body of His glory, by the exertion of the power that He has even to subject all things to Himself.'* Jesus will transform us into beings with bodies suitable for our new heavenly home."

"But what are the benchmarks leading up to the rapture?"

"Simon, old friend, there are many things that have to occur before the rapture, but I think we should always remember that only God the Father knows the exact time. But, there are some interesting benchmarks to look for outlined in Paul's second letter to the Thessalonians. Paul writes, *'Now we request you, brethren, with regard to the coming of our Lord Jesus Christ and our gathering together to Him, that you not be quickly shaken from your composure or be disturbed either by a spirit or a message or a letter as if from us, to the effect that the day of the Lord has come. Let no one in any way deceive you, for it will not come unless the apostasy comes first, and the man of lawlessness is revealed, the son of destruction, who opposes and exalts himself above every so-called god or object of worship, so that he takes his seat in the temple of God, displaying himself as being God. Do you not remember that while I was still with you, I was telling you these things? And you know what restrains him now, so that in his time he will be revealed. For the mystery of lawlessness is already at work; only he who now restrains will do so until he is taken out of the way. Then that lawless one will be revealed whom the Lord will slay with the breath of His mouth and bring to an end by the appearance of His coming; that is, the one whose coming is in accord with the activity of Satan, with all power and signs and false wonders, and with all the deception of wickedness for those who perish, because they did not receive the love of the truth so as to be saved. For this reason God will send upon them a deluding influence so that they will believe what is false, in order that they all may be judged who did not believe the truth, but took pleasure in wickedness.'*

What we should take away from this passage of scripture is that we should not be deceived by anyone or anything that declares when the rapture will take place. It also tells us that after the restraining influence of the Holy Spirit is removed from the world, then the man of lawlessness is revealed; the anti-Christ is revealed. The Holy Spirit will remain until the Church is raptured. So it seems reasonable that the tribulation will most likely occur after the rapture, when the restraining influence of the Holy Spirit is removed. This is what makes the tribulation so terrifying; it's a time of unrestrained evil, unrestrained secular humanism, and unrestrained sin."

"Could Abasi be the lawless one of the Bible? Simon queried.

"If he is, it will be revealed in God's time. But we know he has the potential!"

The sound of a vehicle turning into the Proudman's driveway interrupted the conversation. Geoffrey put his hand on his Ruger 9mm, which was concealed in his waistband. "Who might this be?" He and Simon moved to the open garage door to peer out at the nondescript sedan sitting in the driveway. The driver's door opened and none other than Moishe Silbermann emerged. The passenger's door swung open and Jordan Goldberg disembarked.

"Well, will you look at that!" Geoffrey could hardly believe his eyes.

Simon hurried down the driveway and embraced his old friend. Geoffrey was close behind. After exchanging hugs and backslaps all around, Geoffrey was curious how they had decided to come at such a perfect time. "How did you know we needed you?" Proudman asked.

"Geoffrey, my friend... God has brought us here to the aid of our friends by no small miracle. Getting a flight into the United States was difficult. We had to fly to Europe first, and then into Canada, and then to the United States. Direct flights from Israel are no longer allowed. And, the HSF and TSA are making flights leaving the U.S. even more difficult. Only those bearing the new 'commerce and commodities micro-chip' are able to purchase tickets now; and to get the micro-chip, one must be either atheist or Muslim. The airport is not a safe place for Jews or Christians. They are arresting people by the dozen who are attempting to flee the country for fear of Abasi's anti-Judeo-Christian purge."

"What is this micro-chip?"

"It was just implemented this morning by the Abasi administration. They have stations set up at the ticket counters. If you want to buy a ticket, you have to sign a document renouncing your faith or confirming you are either an atheist or a Muslim. Then you are given an injected micro-chip in your hand or on your forehead; your choice. It leaves a nasty little mark. The talk suggests that very soon you will have to have the micro-chip to buy or sell anything, not just airline tickets."

"It's the mark of the beast," Simon gasped.

"It would seem so," Proudman agreed. "*It also forced all people, great and small, rich and poor, free and slave, to receive a mark on their right hands or on their foreheads, so that they could not buy or sell unless they had the mark, which is the name of the beast or the number of its name. This calls for wisdom. Let the person who has insight calculate the number of the beast, for it is the number of a man. That number is 666.*' That's the last few verses of Revelation 13. The number, 666, in biblical numerology, is the number for humanity, or humanism. And we know that secular humanism is the order of the day."

"We saw hundreds accepting it," Jordan contributed.

"Sadly," Moishe confirmed.

"Well, your timing is perfect, praise God. We are about to relocate to our place in the hill country. And we dare not linger any longer."

"Oh my heavens!" Rachel ran to Simon and Jordan and hugged them both.

"Rachel, Rachel," Moishe smiled warmly at her. "You are a beautiful sight for sore eyes. How are you, my sweet?"

"I am well, all things considered." Rachel's eyes began to tear.

Angelica exited the house from the patio carrying several cloth grocery bags full of supplies. "Oh my gosh! Moishe! Oh, and Jordan! How did you get here? I mean, welcome!" She set the bags down behind the van and ran to hug her friends.

"My word, how simply beautiful you are, Mrs. Proudman! It's true, Jordan... they do make them prettier in Texas!" Moishe was true to form as he hugged Angelica.

"Yes they do!" Jordan agreed taking his turn embracing Angelica.

"I heard about your loss," Moishe said softly to both Angelica and Geoffrey. I can't imagine your pain, but we trust in God that Alex is with our Lord right this moment preparing to greet each of us when we finally make it home."

Geoffrey nodded appreciatively and Angelica hugged him thankfully. Missy, Freddie, C.P. and Hannah arrived at the van, each carrying a bag. Missy ran to Moishe and Jordan and hugged them both.

"Where is the little girl that left us in Israel," Moishe held Missy at arm's length. "She has been replaced by this stunning young woman!" Missy grinned and blushed. "And who are these strapping young lads?"

"That's right, Moishe," Geoffrey responded. "You've never met our sons, Christian Peter and Freddie."

"No I haven't," Moishe said as he extended his hand to each of the young men for a firm handshake. "Ah, good strong grips, the both of you. That's a sign of strength and character!"

"They have that in spades," Geoffrey offered, placing his hands on their shoulders. He paused for a moment and then looked at his watch. "Okay, people. Our time is up here. Does everybody have the essentials?" Proudman looked each person in the eye and all nodded. "Let's load up." Geoffrey made one final sweep of the house and locked the door behind him. Then he did the same to the garage, looking for anything that might be of use. He spotted a Red Cross emergency radio, with a hand-cranked generator built in to it, on the shelf above the work bench. Geoffrey grabbed the radio and shut the garage door, disabling the automatic door opener before he did so. He turned the handle, locking the garage tightly before mounting the driver's seat in the van. Proudman looked back at his passengers and took inventory. C.P. and Hannah were in the last row with an excited Daisy and Coco between them; Missy, Jordan and Moishe were in the next-to-last row; Rachel, Simon and Freddie were in the second row; and Angelica was in the passenger's seat next to him. As he backed down the drive and onto the street he reached for Angelica's hand. Her hand met his and they held onto each other tightly. Geoffrey looked at his wife. Angelica returned his glance and they could see in one another's eyes the same questions... Would they ever again roll into this driveway? Was this the last time they would see their home? They were leaving it all behind; their belongings, their cars, their keepsakes and memories. "It's just stuff," Geoffrey said quietly to Angelica.

"I know. I'm okay." Angelica sighed and blotted a tear from the corner of her eye.

It took considerably longer than usual to reach the Proud-man's hill country home. HSF roadblocks and checkpoints on the main roads forced then to navigate using only county roads and unmapped country dirt tracks to get to their destination. It was dusk by the time they rolled up the long gravel driveway to the house on top of the hill. Geoffrey and Simon disembarked from the van and went to the shed adjacent to the house to turn on the water and power. The rest of the crew unloaded the van and followed Angelica through the front, screened-in porch, and then into the house. The house was nestled between two large pecan trees on top of the dominant hill in the area. The Proudman's property was essentially a 50 acre square, and the hilltop home was at the center on the highest point on the property.

"How long do you think we can stay here?" Simon asked as Geoffrey flipped the main breaker sending electricity into the house and causing the water pump to come to life filling up the tank via the filtration system.

"Well, we are pretty remotely situated out here. It's about 20 miles to the nearest numbered road, so I don't think we will be bothered. The question is, how long should we stay here?"

"Not sure I get the nuance?" Simon responded with a tone of confusion.

"I can't help but think that the rest of our New Covenant family is still back in Houston, trying to avoid exposure to the HSF thugs. I wonder how many are in custody, and in one of the government's "re-education" camps? Shouldn't we be back there helping them?" Geoffrey closed the door to the utility shed.

"I get your meaning. However, you can't just rush in without a plan. Laying low for a few days will give us time to think, pray and formulate a sound tactical response." Simon could see the pain of losing so many of his congregation was starting to bubble to the surface of his friend's conscience.

"I know what you're saying is right," Geoffrey looked his friend squarely in the face, "but I am their Pastor. I can't lead them from here."

"You are also the leader of your family, my friend. Bringing them to safety was the right decision, and you know that to be true because you did it!" Simon put both hands on Geoffrey's shoulders and gripped him firmly. "You did what needed doing. No regrets." Geoffrey nodded. "Right, then!" Simon cuffed Geoffrey's neck. "Good man!"

Simon and Geoffrey entered the house. Moishe was already in the kitchen making pancakes, eggs, and bacon for the crew. Angelica, Missy, Hannah and Rachel were busy putting fresh linens on all the beds. Freddie, C.P. and Jordan decided to walk the property immediately surrounding the house, just to get the lay of the land. Geoffrey poured himself a mug of coffee. Simon did the same. The pair sat at the kitchen table and sipped while Moishe cooked. It wasn't home, but it was warm, dry and smelled like pancakes. Geoffrey thanked God silently for His constant provision.

The kitchen table was not big enough for everyone to sit around together, but the screened-in porch had a long, antique dining room table around which ten could sit comfortably. Suspended from the rafters were two ceiling fans with globe lights, which were probably built in the mid-fifties and still going strong. When set to their lowest speed, they provided just the right circulation to make the mid-September evening meal a pleasant dining experience in the dry Texas hill country heat.

The group gathered around the table as Moishe placed two heaping bowls of scrambled eggs, two stacked platters of steaming pancakes, and two platters of hot, crispy bacon on each end of the long table. Geoffrey extended his hands, one to Angelica on one side, and one to Missy on the other, as he prepared to bless the meal. Everyone followed his example and joined hands with those next to them until the whole group, family and friends, were joined together. Proudman began to pray, "Father God, Jehovah Jireh, our Provider, thank you for delivering us out of the hands of our enemies. And in the midst of our enemies, just as the Psalmist wrote, You have prepared a table before us, and our cups overflow. Bless this food, provided from Your abundance, to the nourishment of our bodies. And may we use that nourishment to strengthen us to serve You in this place. All honor and glory and praise to You, Adonai, in the mighty name of Jesus we pray. Amen."

"Amen." The group responded in unison.

It wasn't long before most of the platters were empty and the ten refugees sat engaging in several conversations around the table. The talk was low-key and careful not to be too heavy or reflective of recent events. When Proudman thought enough time had passed to allow everyone to decompress a bit, he picked up his Bible and his notebook from beside his chair and he began the evening devotional. Proudman was determined to maintain, as much as possible, the practices that had served to bond his family together. Ever since bringing the Morgan kids into his household, he and Angelica had tried to give them the structure and nurture they had spent so much of their youth without. Their natural father had made the effort when they were younger, but when he was killed, the children were left with no spiritual direction. The Proudman's determination to instill regular devotions and worship had paid off, and now all the Proudman kids had grown into strong Christ-followers with rock-solid relationships with Jesus.

"For our devotional this evening," Proudman began and all of the side conversations ceased, "I want to talk about one of my personal Old Testament heroes... David. King David was called a man after God's own heart. He was many things: a shepherd, a musician, a warrior, a psalmist, a preacher of the Word... and a sinner. David did some things in his life that he was not proud of. He took another man's wife and sent her husband into battle to be killed. He sinned against himself, against friends and family, against Israel and against his God. And he suffered painful consequences for his actions. But he is not remembered for his sin because he repented and returned to God, who forgave him, and blotted out his transgressions, and washed him white as snow." Proudman opened his Bible to the center and quickly found his place. "In Psalm 51, David asks God to forgive him, and to remain close to him. He approaches God with a broken and contrite heart and he says to God:

Create in me a clean heart, O God,

And renew a steadfast spirit within me.

Do not cast me away from Your presence

And do not take Your Holy Spirit from me.

Restore to me the joy of Your salvation

And sustain me with a willing spirit.

Then I will teach transgressors Your ways,

And sinners will be converted to You.

I can relate to David. I'm one of those warrior, musician, preacher of the Word, sinner types. Don't know much about sheep, though...But, David and I have some things in common; and I too have things in my past I am not proud of. But, like David, I returned to God and have been washed clean by the crimson blood of Jesus. And like David, I make it my life's work to teach transgressors the way of Christ, so that they will be converted to a relationship with the Father.

The message for those we are trying to bring to Christ is this: 'Beloved, no matter what your past looks like, you too can be restored and redeemed into a right relationship with the Father. The path way to God's mercy and grace is through the Love of Jesus Christ. There is such power in that name. Even the most sordid past can be forgiven. In Him there is no condemnation!'"

"That's beautiful, Geoffrey," Rachel offered.

Geoffrey nodded, acknowledging Rachel's comment. "Thank you, but the words aren't mine; they're Spirit led."

"Yes, but He uses you to deliver them," Rachel insisted.

"Let's talk tactics and strategy," Geoffrey changed the conversation as he felt himself start to blush from the attention.

❧

General Suleimani, President Abasi and Abaddon sat puffing on stogies in the Oval Office while discussing the progress of the Homeland Security Forces in their campaign against the Christians.

"The camps are nearing capacity," Suleimani reported, "with fewer than 30 percent converting to Islam or atheism and earning their release, after receiving the commerce and commodities micro-chip, aka 'the mark.' Of the remaining unconverted 70 percent, three-quarters are put to work producing uniform items for HSF troops and ammunition production, and the last quarter is scheduled for execution via firing squad or guillotine."

"Less than 30 percent converting, General? That's unacceptable!" Abaddon's displeasure was evident. "Obviously you are not pushing the Christians to the breaking point. Step up the pressure. Increase the executions, and make them bloodier. Then we'll see how many of them choose martyrdom over conversion. I want marked people, General! Am I clear? Do I need to do your job for you!?"

"Yes, my Lord! And... no, my Lord."

"And you, my son... what has become of the preacher and those responsible for *The Gathering*? Why are they not wearing my mark or strapped to a guillotine? Do I have to do YOUR job for you too!?"

"No, Father. We are searching for them far and wide using every available means. They have simply vanished."

"I want them, do you understand me. I want their heads. I want their souls. Either will suffice."

Geoffrey laid out an old Greater Houston map on the long dining room table. "We need to think about where our congregation might be if they have been captured."

"I haven't seen one of those in years," Simon remarked. "An actual paper map."

"Not since Google Maps," Geoffrey agreed. "So where in the area surrounding Houston is the most likely place to put an internment camp? I suppose, if I were the government, I could use an existing prison, like Huntsville, but more than likely I would not want to deal with the current residents and an entirely new population of Christian inmates at the same time. So, I would utilize an old FEMA camp or decommissioned military base and convert it to a temporary prison."

"Brilliant. Is there such a place in the vicinity?" Simon queried.

"Well there are two possibilities that come to mind," Geoffrey said thoughtfully. "One is the abandoned FEMA trailer graveyard off of Interstate 45 North. The government dumped several hundred single-wide trailers there after Hurricane Katrina back in 2005. They were never used. The other is an abandoned coast guard facility on Galveston Island. The government refuses to sell the property to land developers. The barracks are dated, but could be converted quickly I assume."

"There's a third option," Angelica chimed in.

"What's your thought?" Geoffrey's curiosity was peaked.

"Where did the Katrina refugees actually end up for a time?" Angelica knew she had the answer to where the Houston-area Christians were being held.

"The Astrodome!" Geoffrey knew she was right on. "Of course. Easily secured and safe from unwanted scrutiny. It's perfect!"

"So what's the plan?" Moishe asked.

"Well, my friend... we need to decide that," Geoffrey responded. "In my mind, we should establish this homestead as our base of operations. Our goal is to liberate Christ-followers from captivity where ever possible. To do that, we will form a band of guerillas and use commando tactics so as not to come head-to-head with the numerically superior and better armed HSF units. We'll be like partisans during WWII. Our goal is not to engage the enemy, but to set the captives free."

"What will we call ourselves?" C.P. was all in.

"Call ourselves?" Geoffrey hadn't expected the question.

"We've got to have a name," C.P. insisted. "All commando units have a name."

"You decide, Son."

"Okay," C.P. was pleased that he got to name the team. "How 'bout... the Conservative Christian Freedom Organization... CCFO for short?"

"CCFO... not bad. Any objections from the rest of the team? No? CCFO it is then." Geoffrey liked the name, but liked that C.P. had taken ownership of it even more. He had been rather reclusive and quiet since watching Cadet Werner die at the hands of the HSF. Proudman hoped he would come around. Maybe getting back into the fight was just what he needed. "Alright then, let's turn in. We'll decide what to do about verifying Angelica's Astrodome theory in the morning. I'll take the first watch; two-hour shifts."

"I'll take the second," C.P. offered.

"Third," Jordan checked-in.

"Last," Freddie decided that he was used to getting up early anyway for cross-country practice.

"Good." Geoffrey poured himself another mug of coffee and went outside to look for a good spot to keep an eye on the perimeter while the rest of the team rested. He decided the treehouse in the biggest of the two pecan trees would give him the best view. He hoped the old ladder and platform were still sturdy enough for him. The structure was there when he and Angelica bought the place and as far as he knew, nobody had ever attempted the ascent. He tested the first rung on the ladder, which appeared sturdy enough. One by one he ascended, surprised to find each rung sound enough to hold him. At the top of the ladder he placed his coffee mug on the platform and pulled himself up, carefully transferring his weight from the ladder to the platform. "So far, so good." He sat on his haunches and looked around him. The view was spectacular. He could see all around the house and down the hill for quite a distance in the moonlight. "This is the spot," he mumbled to himself. He sipped his coffee and settled in for his shift.

About 30 minutes into his watch, Geoffrey saw Angelica emerge from the front porch. He watched as she peered into the moonlit night, obviously looking for him. As she passed below Geoffrey's pecan tree perch, Geoffrey called out to her softly, "Hey hotstuff."

Angelica paused, trying to discern from where Geoffrey's voice came. "Where are you?"

"Look up, Babe."

"Oh, wow. Is that thing safe?"

"It's actually pretty sturdy. Wanna come up?"

"Yes. Is the ladder good?"

"Solid. Come on up."

Angelica pulled herself onto the platform and sat cross-legged next to Geoffrey. "Wow, you can see the whole house and all around for quite a ways."

"Yeah. It's a great look out spot," Geoffrey confirmed. "So, I'm glad you came out, because I need your opinion."

"Okay. About?"

"About whether we should go into Houston and look for ways to help captured Christians. It's obviously dangerous; I mean, just the travel to and from the city would be a great risk. And if we decide that we should do something, who goes and who stays behind? There are a lot of things to consider, not the least of which is the safety of you and our kids."

"Okay, so tell me how you're leaning and then I'll give you my thoughts," Angelica countered.

"Well, I've put some thought and prayer into this and I feel as though standing by and doing nothing is not where I am called to be. What I receive is that I should take action to liberate our people. I also get the sense that each member of our family, each member of our group, must discern their own call here. They are each individual members of the Body of Christ, and with the leading of the Holy Spirit, they should be able to make their own choices. That goes for our kids as well. They are old enough to make that decision for themselves.

What's more, I trust that each of them has a strong relationship with Christ; strong enough to discern their own calling. Your thoughts?"

Angelica sat quietly for a moment before answering, "I agree that we must each decide in what capacity we are led to participate in this effort. I also agree that our kids are capable of their own discernment. I must admit that I am concerned for all of us. But, I am not content to sit idly by and let my New Covenant family, or any Christ-follower for that matter, be held captive, tortured and even killed. My choice is to go with you to try and liberate as many as possible. And I will stand with you in allowing our kids to make up their own minds based on thoughtful prayer and reflection."

"Makes perfect sense to me, Babe." Geoffrey was in a state of constant admiration of Angelica. "You're my favorite human," he mused.

"So I've heard," she responded playfully. She leaned into him and kissed him and then slid quietly down the ladder, leaving Geoffrey craving more of her attention and affection. It was just as well, he thought. He was supposed to be on watch, and Angelica in the moonlight, smelling like *Angel* parfum by Thierry Mugler, his favorite fragrance on her, was a distraction to say the least.

The next morning, as the crew gathered around the table for a hearty bowl of Moishe's brown sugar oatmeal, and some of his hand-pressed sausage patties, Proudman laid out the plan. "So today, we will send a small recon team to check out, in order from north to south, the FEMA trailer graveyard, the Astrodome, and the abandoned Coast Guard facility. Obviously, if we find imprisoned Christians at one of those as we head south, we will stop our southward journey. No need to continue to Galveston if we find what we are looking for at the dome. Once we find prisoners, we must carefully assess the HSF strengths and weaknesses, gather the intel and make our way back here... undetected. Clear?"

"Okay, so who's on the recon team?" Jordan piped up.

"For this trip, me, Simon and Jordan," Proudman answered. Jordan was pleased.

"I know the rest of you want to participate. I can see it in your faces. But, I want each of you to spend some time in prayerful discernment concerning your participation in the actual operation when it's time to liberate our fellow believers. Understood?" The crew nodded. "Good. We leave right after breakfast."

Rachel reached for Simon's hand to get his attention. Simon's attention shifted from his breakfast to his wife. He could see the concern in her eyes and knew what she was about to say before she uttered a word. "Simon, my love... I know better than to try to change your mind about going on this recon thingie, but as your beautiful, caring wife, I must insist that you be extremely careful and not take any unnecessary chances."

"You are, indeed, my beautiful, caring wife. And you are correct in your assessment; my mind is made up about going, but I will heed your advice and keep my head down."

"That's all a beautiful, loving wife can ask." Rachel smiled at her husband. Simon kissed her forehead gently. "Be back before you know it, Love."

chapter

NINE

The Spirit of the Lord God is upon me, because the Lord has anointed me to bring good news to the afflicted; He has sent me to bind up the brokenhearted, to proclaim liberty to captives and freedom to prisoners;

-Isaiah 61:1

Geoffrey, Simon and Jordan mounted up in the white van and rolled down the long driveway to the main road on the edge of the Proudman's 50 acres. They made their way through back roads to a place along the Interstate 45 corridor that intersected the highway close to the old FEMA trailer graveyard. The goal was minimal exposure to the main highway to avoid HSF checkpoints. At the point where they emerged onto the Interstate, they had only about a one-mile stretch on the southbound side feeder road before they reached the FEMA site. As they rolled up on the acres of white trailers, it was evident that it had not been converted to an HSF re-education camp. The place was deserted.

"This place is nothing," Simon remarked.

"It was a shot in the dark," Geoffrey admitted. "Let's get off this Interstate and make our way south to Houston. Next stop, the Astrodome." As Geoffrey spoke, a long column of HSF vehicles rolled past them, headed south on the highway. Geoffrey could feel the hair stand up on his arms and his whole body tingled as the vehicles rolled by. He closed his eyes and prayed that nothing about three men and a white van on the side of the road would arouse the HSF suspicions. He opened his eyes and could not quite comprehend the half dozen Hummers at the end of the column towing what appeared to be trailer-mounted guillotines behind them. After the last vehicle went by, Geoffrey watched as the back of the vehicle got smaller and smaller in the distance. "Did you see what they were towing?"

"Looked like guillotines," Simon said shaking his head disbelievingly.

"Looked that way to me too," Jordan concurred.

"I had hoped I was mistaken," Geoffrey shook his head. "This just went from sinister to diabolical."

"Indeed."

The men had been gone for several hours when Angelica wandered out of the front porch sipping a cup of coffee. As she scanned the beautiful country around her, her mind's eye registered something that looked out of place. She refocused and as she began to comprehend what she was seeing, the coffee cup dropped from her hand as her brain diverted even basic motor skills to fully understanding the magnitude of her circumstances. Just two hundred yards down the hill and closing was an entire platoon of HSF troopers bearing down on the Proudman house.

It was too late to run. All Angelica could do was stand her ground and call for the others to come and stand with her. "Rachel! Come outside please!"

Rachel appeared on the porch and descended the porch steps to stand next to Angelica, holding on to her arm in solidarity. Moishe came out with C.P., Hannah, Missy, and Freddie. C.P. tightened, and Moishe placed a firm hand on his shoulder and gave him one piece of advice. "Hold your tongue and your temper. Understood?"

C.P. nodded.

The HSF troopers surrounded the house and the unit leader approached the group. The leader spoke, "Is this the property of Geoffrey Proudman?"

"It is." Angelica stated matter-of-factly.

"Is Geoffrey Proudman here?"

"No he isn't. He's away. I'm not sure when he'll return."

"We're going to look around. Is there anyone in the house at all?"

"No, we're all right here."

The unit leader signaled for a team to enter the house and they emerged a few minutes later. "It's all clear," the team leader reported.

"What is your name, miss?"

"I am Angelica Proudman. Geoffrey is my husband."

"Well, Mrs. Proudman. I'm placing all of you under arrest and taking you to the Houston processing center for re-education of Christians. This can be a very simple process if you cooperate. Can I count on your cooperation, Mrs. Proudman?"

As Angelica nodded, acknowledging her willingness to go peacefully, several trucks rolled into the yard. The group was cuffed and loaded onto one of the trucks, and the convoy departed within minutes of their arrival. Angelica watched from the back of the truck as everything she called home diminished into the distance. This was the second time in several days she had given up all she had in the world. She thanked God that her true home was yet to be realized.

Geoffrey, Simon and Jordan felt a measure of comfort in the level of anonymity that the traffic in the big city afforded them. There were many white vans around and there was nothing about the three men that advertised their Christianity. Geoffrey felt that if they stayed alert and kept their wits about them, then they should be back in their hill country hideaway by dusk.

Proudman exited the busy loop around the city onto Kirby Drive. The street was filled with mostly HSF vehicles. Proudman could feel the sweat run down his back as he tried his best to look inconspicuous.

"Holy Lord preserve us," Simon uttered as they rolled slowly down the middle of HSF central.

The old Astrodome complex had a new twelve-foot electrified fence surrounding it. The greater Reliant Park, which contained the new stadium and the old dome was now fully under HSF control. The arena complex had been turned into the HSF Southern Command Headquarters. The parking lot was full of black HSF Hummers, trucks, personnel carriers and riot control vehicles. There was an entire squadron of black helicopter gunships and the whole area was well-fortified and patrolled. This was a bite too big to chew for the fledgling CCFO. When the van finally reached the intersection of Kirby and Old Spanish Trail, Proudman let out the breath he had been holding. They sat at the traffic light and watched a convoy of HSF trucks make the turn onto Kirby Drive. Geoffrey's heart sank as the last truck turned and he saw clearly the faces of Angelica and Missy looking out as they passed.

"No! No! No!" Geoffrey blurted out.

"What in blazes?" Simon responded. His nerves already on edge, Geoffrey's sudden outburst made him jump.

"In the truck! Angelica and Missy! They must have raided the house!"

"Are you certain," Simon's heart sank as he thought about Rachel.

"Yes! Absolutely."

Geoffrey made a desperate choice and whipped the van around the median, making an illegal U-turn and followed the truck back up Kirby Drive toward the dome. The truck was only two cars in front of them and Geoffrey could clearly see into the back of it from his driver's seat. Angelica was on the back left side across from Missy on the right. Next to Missy, he could see Freddie and Hannah and C.P. Next to Angelica, he saw Rachel and then Moishe. As the truck approached the turn lane to make the left turn into the HSF complex, Geoffrey pulled right in behind the truck. He looked at Simon in the passenger seat and then back at Jordan on the bench seat behind. "It's now or never. If they get inside, they are gone forever."

Simon nodded agreement; Jordan also. Geoffrey put the van in park and put his hand on the door handle. With the other hand he removed his pistol from the center console. Simon pulled his firearm from the door pocket and Jordan reached into his waistband to retrieve his. "On three," Geoffrey said. "One, Two... Three!" The trio exited the van and walked briskly to the back of the truck. He unlatched the tailgate on one side, while Jordan unlatched the other side. Together they let is down slowly. Angelica and Missy realized what was happening and jumped from the truck to the ground. The two HSF troopers in the back realized what was happening and raised their AK-47s to fire on the escapees. Proudman drilled a double tap into one trooper's forehead while Jordan unloaded three shots into the torso of the second trooper. The rest of Proudman's crew jumped from the truck and all piled into the white van. As Proudman put the van in reverse and hit the gas, he was amazed that they were actually making a go of this. As he jammed the shifter into drive, an HSF riot control vehicle slammed into the driver's door, pushing it into Proudman with such force, he could hear and feel his ribs crack right before his head smacked the door post and he succumbed to the blackness. Their rescue attempt had come to an abrupt and unsuccessful end.

Geoffrey awoke in a stark, institutional, hospital-like room. The florescent lighting units above were surrounded by gray, steel cages. He felt his head. It was tender to the touch and bandaged. He breathed in and stopped short of a full breath because of the stabbing pain in his rib cage. He checked out the room carefully, not moving too much for fear of attracting attention to the fact that he was awake. There was no window in the room and he could see that the door was barred and substantial. A doctor appeared at the barred door and waited for an HSF trooper to unlock it so that he could go inside. He approached Geoffrey's bedside and saw that he was conscious. "How are you feeling, Mr. Proudman?"

"I've been much better." Geoffrey said plainly.

"You've got a mild concussion and a few broken ribs. You'll be sore for a while, but you'll recover... if they allow you the time to do so. Do you know where you are?"

"In an infirmary near the Astrodome complex?"

"Close. Actually you are in the re-education camp infirmary <u>inside</u> the Astrodome. I'm going to release you to the HSF. Try to avoid making them angry. In your condition, you'll be right back in here or worse if you antagonize them."

Geoffrey took a chance that there was some decency in the doctor. He seemed to be a likable fellow. "Doc, are the people that were with me okay?"

"Are they okay? No. They are in an HSF internment camp in the middle of a rundown sports stadium functioning as a prison. I'd say that's pretty far from okay. But, that being said, they are not injured, so that's a silver lining to your dark cloud."

"Thank you," Proudman offered.

The doctor nodded and looked Proudman in the face as if he wanted to say something more, but he turned away toward the barred door and the HSF trooper let him out. "He's ready to go back into the general population. Try to be somewhat civil as you transfer him. He's not 100 percent yet."

The HSF trooper nodded and ordered Proudman to stand and approach the bars. Proudman rose from the bed slowly and walked to the door. "Turn around and put your hands behind your head." Proudman complied, although raising his arms to his head was more than a little painful. The trooper cuffed him and led him out of the hospital cell and down a long corridor. Eventually they emerged onto the stadium field. The sports arena had been converted into a makeshift camp. On one end of the field was row-upon-row of cots. On the other end of the field were several trailer mounted guillotines, a concrete wall suitable for firing squads, a half dozen whipping posts and a large table. Next to that was a bigger-than-life portrait of President Abasi, and next to that a massive screen for showing re-education videos, which currently displayed the HSF insignia. Below the logo was projected the usual slogan, *"There is no god but Allah, and Muhammad is Allah's prophet."*

The prisoners were clustered in the center of the field. Proudman estimated there were about 600 of them, more or less; men, women and children. There was no attempt by the

HSF to separate them by sex, age or any other division. They were simply herded together, like cattle.

The trooper stopped Proudman at the edge of the field and removed the handcuffs. He gestured toward the herd of prisoners and Proudman cautiously walked toward the crowd. How would he ever find Angelica and the rest of his people? He walked the perimeter of the crowd first, looking for a familiar face. The faces he saw were haggard and defeated. Their eyes were dull and lifeless and they looked devoid of hope. As he moved around the mass of people a male voice called to him from somewhere in the crowd, "Pastor! Pastor Proudman!" Geoffrey searched for the source and his eyes came to rest on a familiar face; it was Jim Clancy from the New Covenant Church vestry.

"Jim! Good to see a familiar face. How are you?"

"Not too bad considering. You okay? You've looked better, I must say."

"I'm going to make it. Have you seen any of my family, Jim?"

"Saw your wife and daughter and your friend, Rachel, not 30 minutes ago, over that way. But you better hurry because it's almost time for the next education session and they really don't like anyone to be moving around and not paying attention while those are going on. Marci didn't pay attention to the first one, you remember my wife, Marci, don't you?"

"Of course I remember Marci, Jim."

"Yes, well... Marci was talking to me about something, you know how she liked to talk... anyway she was telling me something and before I knew it, Marci was up on one of those trailers and they cut her head clean off. You remember my wife Marci, don't you Pastor... she ought to be along here any minute."

It was then Geoffrey realized he wasn't having a conversation with Jim Clancy, but a shell-shocked version of the former man. Jim was babbling on and on about Marci, one moment aware of her demise, the next moment expecting her to join them in conversation. "Jim, why don't you sit down here and take a load off while I go find Angelica. Okay?"

"Take a load off, that's just what I'll do. Marci should be along any minute now. Don't know what's keeping her. You go find your wife before they start the next session. But pay attention, Pastor, or they might take her head."

Geoffrey shuddered as he walked away from Jim. He thought he would come back at some point and find Jim after he located his family. He wanted to help Jim deal with Marci's death, but his priority had to be finding Angelica and his children. He went in the direction Jim had pointed and after about 10 minutes of searching, he felt arms wrap around him from behind. He winced at the pain in his rib cage, but when he realized that it was Missy hugging him, he didn't care about the pain for long. "Missy! Where are the others?" he asked while clinging to his daughter.

"They're right over here. Everyone is here. They only one we were missing was you." Missy led Geoffrey by the hand over to an area close to the sidelines. There in a circle were Angelica, Rachel, C.P., Freddie, Hannah, Jordan, Simon and Moishe. All present and accounted for. As he embraced Angelica, a chime sounded, much like someone was announcing that the show was about to start at a Broadway musical.

"Come! Standup and face the screen and don't talk!" Angelica instructed. The entire mass of people instantly stopped talking, stood and faced the screen. Proudman watched as his family and friends followed suit. The lights dimmed and the screen came to life with a video of President Abasi working his way through a crowd of adoring Americans, waving flags and cheering as he shook hands and kissed babies. As he entered the White House, the video depicted him turning back toward the adoring crowd and waving to them with a big smile on his face. As the doors shut behind him, the video faded and then transitioned to Abasi sitting behind his desk at the Oval Office. The camera moved in tighter on Abasi's over-sized head and he began to speak.

"My fellow Americans, it is time for you to put away two thousand years of false teaching and hate speech in the Christian Church, and many more thousands of years of the same in the practice of Judaism. These hateful religions will no longer be tolerated in the New America. As I move this nation into a harmonious alliance with other nations to create a New World Order, there simply will be no room for multiple religions, especially those inherently devoid of tolerance, diversity and inclusion. So, going forward, there will be only one religion allowed in the New America; that being the religion of peace, the religion of the one true deity, Allah. From now on, only the religion of Islam will be allowed. Alternatively, you may choose the religion of unbelief, atheism.

In order to leave the re-education camp in which you find yourself today, you must do three very important things. First, you must renounce your belief in God, Jesus, the Holy Spirit and all such icons of the Judeo-Christian tradition. Secondly, you must confess your faith in Islam by reciting the Shahada, *'There is no god but Allah, and Muhammad is Allah's prophet.'* Or you may sign the record of non-belief as an atheist. Thirdly, you must pledge your allegiance to me by having the commodities and commerce micro-chip, commonly known as *the mark*, injected into your hand or forehead. Do these three things and you will be allowed to return to your homes unharmed. Do them not and you will taste the wrath of the HSF Camp Commandant's whip, or worse, at his discretion. Choose wisely, because I have given each Camp Commandant the full authority to pronounce capital sentencing on all refusing to cooperate."

The video ended and a squad of HSF troopers herded a dozen prisoners up to the concrete wall. The squad leader stepped in front of the first prisoner, held a microphone to his face and asked him if he wanted to renounce his faith and accept *the mark*. The terrified man shook his head quickly. "You have to say the words," the trooper advised him with an attitude of annoyance.

"I renounce my faith and choose Islam," he said shakily. An EMT stepped forward with a large hypodermic device and said flatly, "Head or hand?"

The man looked confused, so the EMT asked him a second time; this time poking the man roughly with his pointer finger in the places indicated. "Head or hand?"

The man finally understood what was about to happen and he balked. "No, I can't take that! I'll go to hell when I die."

The squad leader didn't hesitate. He removed his baton from his belt and drove it into the man's stomach, causing him to crumple at the squad leader's feet. Two troopers moved in and dragged the breathless man to one of the trailer mounted guillotines. They strapped the man down as he began to panic, realizing what was about to happen. The blade was raised with the whirr of an electric motor. It clicked into place about eight feet in the air between the side-rails of the machine. The man was moved into position manually by a trooper on one side of the machine's deck, where the man was strapped, face-down. The operator pulled a lever and the deck locked into place and a collar closed around the man's neck, which held the man's head into a position suspended over a metal basket. The trooper pulled another lever and the blade accelerated down the channels until it severed the terrified man's head from his body. Worker's in jumpsuits removed the body and the head and carted them away. The process repeated until the remaining eleven people either chose to be re-educated or executed. Following the dozen choosers, those prisoners the HSF determined hadn't paid attention well enough, were put to death. If there were just a few, they were strapped under the blade. If there were more than a few, they were put against the wall and shot. As Proudman watched the horrifying spectacle, he saw that one of the half dozen of those who hadn't

paid close enough attention to the session was Jim Clancy. Proudman prayed and wept as Jim took a firing squad's bullets, rejoin-
ing Marci after only an hour or so of separation.

A buzzer sounded indicating the end of the session. The
crowd seemed relieved as workers brought in boxes of MREs and
began distributing the brown plastic bags of rations to the prisoners. The evening meal signaled the end of sessions for the day.
Proudman and the crew sat together on a group of cots and began
to open their MREs. No one spoke at first. Each sat nibbling at
a cracker or some other component of the meal, trying to digest
what was happening to them and the people around them. Angelica spoke first. "I know that when my time comes, I will not
renounce my Savior and I will not take *the mark*. Is there anyone
who doubts that they will be able to stand firm in their faith?"

Geoffrey followed up on Angelica's question. "Angelica
asks a valid and important question. Is there anyone among us
that feels they are weak in this circumstance? Speak now so that
we can deal with it."

Rachel squeezed Simon's hand tightly and offered, "I must
admit that I am afraid. Not of dying, exactly, because I know
where I am going. But I'm afraid of the pain and suffering I
must endure to get there. The thought of that thing chopping
my head off or a bullet tearing into me scares me so..." Simon
held her hand even more firmly.

"I understand, Rachel," Geoffrey looked her squarely in the
face. "Remember what Paul says, *'Therefore we do not lose heart, but*

though our outer man is decaying, yet our inner man is being renewed day by day. For momentary, light affliction is producing for us an eternal weight of glory far beyond all comparison, while we look not at the things which are seen, but at the things which are not seen; for the things which are seen are temporal, but the things which are not seen are eternal.' That's 2 Corinthians 4:16-18. Even something as extreme as that horrible machine is only temporary. It is but a blink of an eye in the grand scheme of eternity. By saying yes to Jesus, you assure your future with Him in heaven. Hold fast to that and you will make it to the other side of all this. I promise!" Rachel nodded. "So here's what we need to do. After you eat something to keep your strength and wits about you, we need to very quietly split up and go around to the rest of these people. I want the ten of us, solid in our stand for Christ, to minister to this congregation of prisoners. Reinforce the gospel message in their hearts; share the love and hope of Christ with them; and tell them the message I shared just now with Rachel... this is but a momentary, light affliction producing for us an eternal weight of glory!"

The group felt energized. They suddenly had a purpose again. To help these people make the right choice in the face of certain death. They might not avoid the transition, but they could control the destination!

The following morning, there was a strange atmosphere in the Astrodome. As the morning MREs were distributed, Proudman noticed that there were more HSF troopers around than usual and they were all wearing dress uniforms instead of the usual daily uniforms. The platform where the re-education took place was adorned with large black and red HSF banners, and the squad leaders and officers were barking more orders than usual. Proudman thought back to his Marine Corps days and muttered, "Dignitaries."

"Come again," Simon said as Geoffrey took a bite of spaghetti and meat balls from his MRE.

"All the trimmings and dress uniforms can only mean one thing... someone important is coming to visit today. Be on your toes."

As Proudman predicted, before the morning meal time was over, the HSF began roughly pushing prisoners into ranks and files instead of the usual cluster in the middle of the stadium's field. As the morning session's chime sounded, a black limousine flying the American flag on one side and the HSF flag on the other pulled parallel to the re-education pad. A trooper opened the rear door and saluted as General Qassim Suleimani exited and was greeted by the Camp Commandant. The two hardly had time for a few pleasantries when a second limousine pulled up to the platform and came to a stop. The trooper once again held the door and saluted as President Anwar Abasi stepped out. The General and the Commandant gave crisp salutes and then shook Abasi's hand as they toured the platform. Abasi nodded approvingly at the trailer-mounted guillotines, carefully looking them over with interest. He then gestured animatedly at his larger-than-life portrait and ran his gloved hand over the Shahada image projected onto the large screen.

"Well done Commandant," Abasi complimented. Turning to Suleimani, he queried, "So what percentage of these prisoners will choose *the mark* General?"

"Our techniques are proving effective around the country, Excellency. If this group is anything like the national average, we should see almost eighty percent conversion during the session this morning." Suleimani was proud of his program.

"Eighty percent, you say. Impressive. Well let's see if that holds true, General." The dignitaries moved to a private skybox to watch the events on closed circuit television.

The General turned to the Commandant, who turned to his second and after a few rungs down the ladder of command, HSF troopers shoved a dozen prisoners against the concrete wall and began the process. One by one, each of the twelve stood firm in their faith and went under the blade. Somewhat embarrassed the Commandant ordered another session immediately. Another group of twelve was ushered to the wall and each one in turn chose Jesus and the blade. "I assure you Mr. President, this is a fluke." The Commandant ordered a third session. The troopers rounded up a dozen more and took them to the whipping posts. They flogged them until they were bloodied and broken and then herded them against the wall to make their choice. Again the twelve, each in turn, chose Christ and death by guillotine.

General Suleimani took the Commandant aside and admonished him angrily, "You are making me look like a fool! Why is no one converting?"

"I don't know, General. Yesterday we were better than eighty-five percent in conversions!"

"Well get me another dozen and this time we had better see some new Muslims or atheists walk away! Understood?"

"Yes, General."

The Commandant nervously issued the order for yet another session to take place. Another dozen people were marched in front of the wall and all of them stood firm in their faith. The frustrated squad leader ordered the dozen martyrs to be shot rather than continue to grease the rails of the guillotines.

The Commandant, red-faced and humiliated, began to grovel in front of General Suleimani who brushed him aside so that he himself could grovel in front of President Abasi. In the midst of all the groveling, Abaddon manifested and placed his pale white hand over the Commandant's overflowing mouth. The Commandant stopped in mid-grovel as Abaddon continued to apply cheek-bone crushing pressure to the man's face. He screamed in pain as Abaddon tore away the Commandant's jaw and dropped it to the floor. The Commandant soon followed it, and as he writhed in pain at Abaddon's feet, Abaddon placed his foot on the helpless man's skull and crushed it with little exerted effort. Suleimani's groveling stopped and he bowed his head, trying to avoid eye-contact with Abaddon.

"Fools!" Abaddon growled. "You are imbeciles, all of you! Can't you see that you have someone in your camp that is giving them the one thing that guarantees a choice for their faith? Someone is sharing the hope of Christ with them! Find out who that is and kill him... messily, bloodily, publically. That's how you stop this nonsense!"

"Yes, Father. But who is the culprit? How do we identify him?"

Abaddon went to the window of the skybox and gazed down onto the field. He could feel the presence of the Holy Spirit in the stadium and he drew back from the glass in fear. "This is worse than I thought," he admitted. Abaddon noticed the closed circuit television. "Have them pan the prisoners slowly." In a few moments the camera began a slow pan, row by row, column by column. The camera panned over Simon and Geoffrey and Rachel and Angelica and continued down the row. "Stop! Tell them to go back slowly!" The camera panned back the other way, Angelica, Rachel, Geoffrey..."Stop! It's them. The preacher and the archaeologist and their wives! First *The Gathering* and then Hakeldama and now this! But not this time, Priest! This time I've got you!"

The General ordered Geoffrey and his group be ushered to the wall, while he, Abasi and Abaddon made their way to the field. "Stay calm and stay strong," Geoffrey encouraged. But their hearts sank when Abaddon walked onto the platform and face to face with Geoffrey.

"So, Priest. We are together again." Abaddon breathed his hate into Geoffrey's face. "Not so smug this time, though. Are we?"

Geoffrey chose not to respond and simply raised his eyes toward heaven. Abaddon looked skyward and snarled. "No God will save you this time, Priest." Abaddon motioned for the squad leader to take Geoffrey to a whipping post to be scourged. Two HSF troopers shoved and kicked Geoffrey into position in front of a post and chained his hands high above his head, forcing him to either hang from his wrists or stand uncomfortably on his toes. The troopers went to the wooden table and picked up one cat-o-nine-tails each. Angelica gasped as she saw the menacing instruments, each with nine whips braided with bits of glass and metal for ripping flesh. The two troopers alternated horrific blows across Geoffrey's back. Blow after blow, the fabric of his shirt disintegrated and his skin with it, until forty-odd lashes later, the scourging ended. Angelica wept quietly. Missy had closed her eyes and put her hands over her ears in an attempt to block out the sound of the lashes. She opened her eyes and was overwhelmed by the bloody mess that once was her dad. She collapsed and an HSF trooper kicked her twice until he realized that she wasn't getting up.

The troopers then dragged Proudman to the nearest guillotine and strapped him to the deck. Proudman prayed through the pain, and supernaturally, through the power of the Holy Spirit, his voice was amplified throughout the stadium, "Abba, Father, I am not worthy to have been scourged in the manner of my Savior. I praise Your Holy Name and commend my spirit to Your loving hands. Take me into Your presence, by the blood of Jesus, and grant Father that all of these, my family and friends who follow me today, believers all, will be with You today in paradise. In Jesus mighty Name I pray!" Proudman's voice echoed across the field.

It was then that Geoffrey heard it. In the very moment his voice was crying out to God, while the blade reached maximum velocity along its 8-foot long track, the distinct blast of a magnificent trumpet sounded. It was more than sound; it permeated the ground and the air with an intense pulse of vibration. It was not so much heard as it was felt. In the split-second of the trumpet's call, Proudman's body vanished from the machine's deck, leaving nothing but his bloody, tattered shirt, trousers and shoes behind; and the deadly blade impacted against the stops without ever passing through Proudman's neck. Geoffrey sensed that he was rising rapidly. The guillotine and the camp quickly faded in the distance below him and Geoffrey immediately felt his physical body transform, from sense to soul, into a stronger, faster, sleeker, version of himself. He radiated light. He felt grace. He felt warmth and peace and love. He looked, and all around him were people rising along with him. He realized he knew them, all of them, thousands of them, by name. His thoughts went to Angelica, and suddenly before him, there she was. She was more radiant than ever and she smiled at him and took his hand so that they rose together, higher and higher into the clouds and beyond.

As Geoffrey thought of each of his family members, they too appeared near him. There were C.P. and Hannah, also hanging on to one another as they glided heavenward; and Simon and Rachel, and Moishe, and Jordan, and Freddie, each streaking skyward in transformed, glorified bodies. Missy flew near to Geoffrey and Angelica, her face beaming as she flicked her wrist or her foot to change direction and spiraled upward, maneuvering as if she had been flying like this her whole life. Behind her was what Geoffrey could only surmise was an angel, desperately trying to keep up with her. It was then that he noticed an angel by his side and another by Angelica, each there to welcome and escort them into their heavenly home. It appeared everyone had an angel escort to greet them.

Geoffrey noticed that their ascent had slowed and the vapor around them subsided to reveal a beautiful panoramic scene of green grasslands, gentle hills, lush vegetation, fragrant flowers and clear rivers of sparkling water. It was like the earth, only more vivid and fresh, and it stretched before them as far as their eyes could see. Geoffrey turned to his escort angel and spoke his first words in his glorified body, "Is this heaven?" His voice had never sounded so clear and resonant before. He smiled, pleased with the sound.

The angel smiled back at him, "Yes. This is your new home, at least until the new heaven and the new earth are ready for the return of the Son. All your questions will be answered in the fullness of time, but now you must prepare to meet the Groom." The angel produced a brilliant, seamless white robe and motioned for Geoffrey to put it on. Geoffrey could see that all of the people were receiving robes like his. Angelica pulled hers on over her head. She looked glorious, like a bride. As the people donned their garments, a trumpet sounded. "Run to the Son," the angels told their charges. "Run and meet the Son of Man, the Groom!"

Geoffrey grasped Angelica's hand. He looked around for their children, and seeing them appear near him in the instant he thought of them, he called out to them, "Come on! Let's go meet Jesus!" The people began to run, thousands and thousands of them, moving like gazelles over fields and hills, valleys and streams. They ran, but did not get weary. They ran effortlessly, covering great distances in no time at all. Simon and Rachel laughed as they went. Joy moved them forward in great anticipation of finally seeing their Savior face to face.

A brilliant light appeared on a distant hill; more radiant than anything else in view. The people surrounded the hill and looked to its peak at their glorious Lord settling down upon it. As if on cue, the people sat expectantly. Jesus motioned for the Book and an angel set the great volume down before Him. He opened it and read the first name. A woman on the hillside rose and then appeared directly in front of Jesus. As she stood there, face to face with Christ, every word, every deed, every nuance of her life played before the multitude. The woman laughed at times, cried at others, and hung her head when things were revealed that were less than flattering. When it was all said and done, Jesus embraced her, spoke softly into her ear, and she returned to the hillside to watch the rest of the people go before the King.

In no time, Proudman heard his Lord call him out. No sooner had he gotten to his feet, he found himself looking directly into the eyes of Jesus. As he gazed upon the Savior, his life began to play before him. The entire timeline unfolded before the multitude and all present could see everything that Jesus saw. Geoffrey saw his childhood and the selfish teenage years, he saw the times he was disobedient to his parents and his God. He saw his failed marriage play out before Christ, and he saw his Christ-centered marriage to Angelica; what a difference there was between the two with Christ in the middle. He saw his combat years and he felt the forgiveness pour over him for every life he had taken. He hung his head in shame at every wicked thought, every unrighteous act he had ever committed. And he saw his faith emerge, his salvation moment, his ordination, and his ministry unfold. When his life story had been spent in the presence of the Master, Geoffrey found himself on his knees in front of Jesus. He could not control the sobs of sorrow and pain that emerged from his heart as it emptied onto the ground at Christ's feet. He wished with all his heart that he could take back every sin that had driven the nails into his Master's hands and feet. Jesus gently placed a hand on each of his shoulders and guided Geoffrey up, off of his knees. "Stand up my child," Jesus said softly. With His hands gently on Geoffrey's cheeks, the Messiah wiped the tears away from the corners of his eyes. "Do not cry, Geoffrey," Jesus said. "You are home and I have wiped the tears away. Your sins are forgiven and cast away, as far as the east is from the west, and I will remember them no more forever."

Jesus looked to the multitude and said, "All who came to me because of this man's teaching, rise." One-by-one, those present at *The Gathering* stood along the hillside, and all of those from New Covenant Church, and many from the television broadcast, and many more from the supernatural reach of the Holy Spirit working through Geoffrey's years of ministry. And there were those from the camp who had listened to his words in stolen moments in the midst of the brutality; words of hope eternal in the arms of Christ. When the last person rose, they all shouted in unison, "Halleluiah, halleluiah, halleluiah!" Geoffrey faced his Lord again, overwhelmed with joy. Jesus produced a crown of gold and placed it on Geoffrey's head saying, "Well done, good and faithful servant!" Geoffrey reached up and touched the crown, and then he went to his knees once again, kissing Jesus' feet. Geoffrey removed the crown from his head, and laid it before Jesus, giving God the glory for all He had done. Jesus touched his head where the crown had been and looked into Geoffrey's face with a smile. Instantly Geoffrey was back in his place on the hillside. Joyfully he watched Angelica receive a crown, and Simon, Rachel, Moishe, and Jordan, each receiving the crown of righteousness for their part in spreading the Gospel of Jesus Christ.

In what seemed like no time at all, every person had gone before Jesus. When the last person had watched their life play out, the angel escorts came and ushered all of them into a great hall. The structure appeared to be white marble and alabaster with accents of pure gold. There was no roof, but the blue sky was perfectly cloudless. The windows appeared to be translucent gold and the floor was a black and white porcelain tile in a checkerboard pattern reminiscent of Solomon's temple. Stretching into the distance was a long banquet table filled to overflowing with foods of every variety. There were grapes as large as plums and plums as large as grapefruit. There were breads and all manner of sumptuous fare. At the head of the table sat the Groom, Christ Himself. Remarkably, no matter where one sat, the view to Jesus was intimate and personal. "Welcome, my bride, my Church, to the wedding feast of the Lamb!" A great cheer went up among the people and the feast began. The angels peered in to the great hall through the open roof and sang, "Holy, Holy, Holy is the Lord God, the Almighty, who was and who is and who is to come."

After the feast, Geoffrey and the group found themselves together under a great tree outside the hall. The grass was like a thick, deep green carpet, and as Geoffrey sat on it, he could not get over how perfectly green and comfortable it was. The tree's roots fed from a clear stream next to it, and the stream rambled through the countryside and disappeared into the hills beyond.

"It's so beautiful here," Angelica sighed.

"It is more beautiful than I ever could have imagined," Rachel agreed.

Missy's eyes followed the stream into the distance and her heart voiced what she was feeling, "What do you suppose will happen to those we left behind, Dad?"

The entire group tuned into Geoffrey as he contemplated Missy's question carefully. "Well, Missy... in the instant we were raptured, the Great Tribulation began on Earth, just as was written in the Book of Revelation. The tribulation will last for 7 years during which God will pour out judgment on those remaining on the earth. Beginning with the Seven Seal Judgments, then the Seven Trumpet Judgments, then the Seven Bowl Judgments, each judgment brings death and destruction, in God's perfect justice, to an unbelieving world. The world will see the rise and defeat of the Antichrist, and all of that ends with Armageddon; when Christ, in His Glorious Appearing, and we along with Him, return to claim Earth where Christ will rule as King."

"Will any survive the Tribulation," Freddie asked hopefully.

"Some will endure and receive Christ, but it will be extremely difficult because when we rose to meet Christ, the Holy Spirit came with us. He no longer resides with the people left behind, so there are no barriers at all now preventing Satan from doing whatever he will in the hearts and minds of people still in the world."

As they discussed, two women approached the group and stood patiently on the edge of their circle. Jordan's face beamed as he slowly stood and approached one of the women. "Miriam!" Jordan could not believe his eyes. She smiled back at him and hugged his neck and kissed his cheek gently.

"I want to thank you for helping my parents through my death," Miriam said. "They are here now and would like to spend some time catching up with you... with us... later." Jordan nodded.

Moishe stood and Miriam ran to him and hugged him. "It has been an eternity since I've seen that smile," Moishe said to her. "And who is this with you?"

The second woman pulled the hood of her robe down and shook out her long, flowing hair. Simon took a deep breath as Sarah's face shown radiantly down on him as he sat in the grass next to Rachel. "Rachel," Simon said softly, "this is Sarah, my first wife." Rachel rose and Sarah embraced her as a sister in Christ. She then hugged Simon and nodded approvingly at his choice in Rachel.

As everyone got reacquainted and caught up, Missy noticed a young man approaching the group. She knew the walk and the way he carried himself, but in her wildest imagination, she could not have conceived of this reunion. It had to be Alex. Only Angelica noticed when Missy put her hands to her mouth in total surprise, and then got up and ran toward the young man. "Look!" Angelica pointed as Missy embraced her brother. "It's Alex!" All took their turn hugging their newly found family member.

Geoffrey wandered along the bank of the stream a short distance away from the happy reunion taking place underneath the great tree. He watched the water dance over the rocky bottom of the stream and followed a school of brightly colored fish as they darted to and fro. The warmth of the light surrounded him and Geoffrey thanked God for His promises. Heaven was everything God's Word said it would be. His Words were true! Geoffrey searched his mind for a fitting verse to describe what he was experiencing. And God smiled and placed this word on his heart: *"He will swallow up death for all time, And the Lord God will wipe tears away from all faces, And He will remove the reproach of His people from all the earth; For the Lord has spoken."* (Isaiah 25:8)

AFTERWORD

The Love of Jesus is calling you right now. God's Grace and Mercy are being extended to you at this very moment. The question, beloved, is how will you respond. The message God is sending to you now is the good news of the gospel. It is a simple message. So simple, in fact, that the only people who do not get it are those that <u>choose</u> not to respond to it. My guess is that if you are a seeker and have read everything in this book up to this point, then you are still able to receive what God is offering. But time is short, so please don't tarry as you ponder where to go from here.

The gospel message is simply this: As human beings we are living in a state of being that is far less than the perfection God created for us. Because of sin, the lives we lead now fall short of

God's mark, no matter what we do. We are sinners incapable of earning or working our way out of our sinful state.

God's desire is to be reconciled with us because, despite our sin, God loves us. But, because He is Holy, He cannot be in fellowship with us and our sin. The sin must be removed. Because God is Holy, He is perfectly just. His justice demands that our sin be paid for in blood. The cost of sin is death.

God's plan to redeem us was to send His only begotten Son, Jesus, into the world as a human being. He was born into flesh, grew up, and became a man. Upon entering into His earthly ministry, He was tempted by Satan and the ways of the world, the same temptations that afflict us today, yet He remained perfectly sinless. Having accomplished a sinless life, He became the perfect substitute for our sins; a perfect, unblemished sacrifice. And so He chose to take all of our sins to the cross with Him; and on the cross, Jesus died for us. But He didn't stop there. He went to the grave and three days later, He arose and was seen by many witnesses. Jesus conquered death so that we could be spared that eternal separation from God. All we have to do is believe on Him and accept Him as Lord of our life, and we too will take part in that resurrection.

The next part of the message is somewhat inconvenient if you are sitting on the fence, wondering what to do with all of this salvation talk. And because I want the language to be as plain as the nose on my face, I chose <u>The Message</u> version of the Bible for this part of our discussion. Beloved, Jesus is coming soon. And when he comes, He will sort out the people into two groups... Christ-followers and everyone else. At that point, all of the arguments for tolerance, diversity, universality, inclusion, etc. will be null and void. For those who insist on perpetuating the lie that all religions are the same and that everyone can find their own way to heaven, on their own terms... it will be GAME OVER.

Heed the following passage from Matthew 25. Consider carefully that your pride, your false (humanistic) sense of justice and equality, all of those things that the world says are right, are worthless rags compared to the Holy Righteousness of God. It is an inconvenient truth, but truth nonetheless.

After Christ's Glorious Appearing, His second advent, the Bible describes the future event known as the Sorting of the Sheep and the Goats in Matthew 25. It says, *"When he finally arrives, blazing in beauty and all his angels with him, the Son of Man will take his place on his glorious throne. Then all the nations will be arranged before him and he will sort the people out, much as a shepherd sorts out sheep and goats, putting sheep to his right and goats to his left.*

Then the King will say to those on his right, 'Enter, you who are blessed by my Father! Take what's coming to you in this kingdom. It's been ready for you since the world's foundation. And here's why:

I was hungry and you fed me,

I was thirsty and you gave me a drink,

I was homeless and you gave me a room,

I was shivering and you gave me clothes,

I was sick and you stopped to visit,

I was in prison and you came to me.'

"Then those 'sheep' are going to say, 'Master, what are you talking about? When did we ever see you hungry and feed you, thirsty and give you a drink? And when did we ever see you sick or in prison and come to you?' Then the King will say, 'I'm telling the solemn truth: Whenever you did one of these things to someone overlooked or ignored, that was me—you did it to me.'

"Then he will turn to the 'goats,' the ones on his left, and say, 'Get out, worthless goats! You're good for nothing but the fires of hell. And why? Because—

I was hungry and you gave me no meal,

I was thirsty and you gave me no drink,

I was homeless and you gave me no bed,

I was shivering and you gave me no clothes,

Sick and in prison, and you never visited.'

"Then those 'goats' are going to say, 'Master, what are you talking about? When did we ever see you hungry or thirsty or homeless or shivering or sick or in prison and didn't help?'

"He will answer them, 'I'm telling the solemn truth: Whenever you failed to do one of these things to someone who was being overlooked or ignored, that was me—you failed to do it to me.'

"Then those 'goats' will be herded to their eternal doom, but the 'sheep' to their eternal reward." (Matthew 25: 31-46)

That account in Matthew 25 is pretty straight forward. Are you one of the Lord's sheep, or are you a goat? There is a Hell and it is waiting to receive those who reject the free gift of salvation. Jesus Christ is the way, the truth and the life. No one comes to the Father, but by Him.